MW00333091

TO DIE FOR

EVA RAE THOMAS MYSTERY - BOOK 8

WILLOW ROSE

Copyright © Willow Rose 2021
Published by BUOY MEDIA LLC
All rights reserved.

No part of this book may be reproduced, scanned, or distributed in
any printed or electronic form without permission from the author.

This is a work of fiction. Any resemblance of characters to actual
persons, living or dead is purely coincidental. The Author holds
exclusive rights to this work. Unauthorized duplication is prohibited.

Cover design by Juan Villar Padron,
https://www.juanjpadron.com

Special thanks to my editor Janell Parque
http://janellparque.blogspot.com/

Books by the Author

HARRY HUNTER MYSTERY SERIES

- All The Good Girls
- Run Girl Run
- No Other Way
- Never Walk Alone

MARY MILLS MYSTERY SERIES

- What Hurts the Most
- You Can Run
- You Can't Hide
- Careful Little Eyes

EVA RAE THOMAS MYSTERY SERIES

- Don't Lie to me
- What you did
- Never Ever
- Say You Love me
- Let Me Go
- It's Not Over
- Not Dead yet
- To Die For

EMMA FROST SERIES

- Itsy Bitsy Spider
- Miss Dolly had a Dolly
- Run, Run as Fast as You Can
- Cross Your Heart and Hope to Die
- Peek-a-Boo I See You

- TWEEDLEDUM AND TWEEDLEDEE
- EASY AS ONE, TWO, THREE
- THERE'S NO PLACE LIKE HOME
- SLENDERMAN
- WHERE THE WILD ROSES GROW
- WALTZING MATHILDA
- DRIP DROP DEAD
- BLACK FROST

JACK RYDER SERIES

- HIT THE ROAD JACK
- SLIP OUT THE BACK JACK
- THE HOUSE THAT JACK BUILT
- BLACK JACK
- GIRL NEXT DOOR
- HER FINAL WORD
- DON'T TELL

REBEKKA FRANCK SERIES

- ONE, TWO…HE IS COMING FOR YOU
- THREE, FOUR…BETTER LOCK YOUR DOOR
- FIVE, SIX…GRAB YOUR CRUCIFIX
- SEVEN, EIGHT…GONNA STAY UP LATE
- NINE, TEN…NEVER SLEEP AGAIN
- ELEVEN, TWELVE…DIG AND DELVE
- THIRTEEN, FOURTEEN…LITTLE BOY UNSEEN
- BETTER NOT CRY
- TEN LITTLE GIRLS
- IT ENDS HERE

MYSTERY/THRILLER/HORROR NOVELS

- SORRY CAN'T SAVE YOU
- IN ONE FELL SWOOP

- UMBRELLA MAN
- BLACKBIRD FLY
- TO HELL IN A HANDBASKET
- EDWINA

HORROR SHORT-STORIES

- MOMMY DEAREST
- THE BIRD
- BETTER WATCH OUT
- EENIE, MEENIE
- ROCK-A-BYE BABY
- NIBBLE, NIBBLE, CRUNCH
- HUMPTY DUMPTY
- CHAIN LETTER

PARANORMAL SUSPENSE/ROMANCE NOVELS

- IN COLD BLOOD
- THE SURGE
- GIRL DIVIDED

THE VAMPIRES OF SHADOW HILLS SERIES

- FLESH AND BLOOD
- BLOOD AND FIRE
- FIRE AND BEAUTY
- BEAUTY AND BEASTS
- BEASTS AND MAGIC
- MAGIC AND WITCHCRAFT
- WITCHCRAFT AND WAR
- WAR AND ORDER
- ORDER AND CHAOS
- CHAOS AND COURAGE

THE AFTERLIFE SERIES

- BEYOND
- SERENITY
- ENDURANCE
- COURAGEOUS

THE WOLFBOY CHRONICLES

- A GYPSY SONG
- I AM WOLF

DAUGHTERS OF THE JAGUAR

- SAVAGE
- BROKEN

Is it true?
    That the pain inside of me could be you?
    Kings Garden by Tim Christensen, Danish singer

Prologue
VIERA, FLORIDA

It was just one of those days. Sarah Abbey was late for work at the Bed Bath & Beyond in The Avenues due to a traffic accident. Her clients, a young engaged couple who wanted to register there, were upset from the beginning because she was late for their appointment. It ruined the atmosphere, and the groom-to-be didn't like any of Sarah's ideas. They ended up leaving without registering, and Sarah's entire morning was wasted. Then, at lunch, she realized she had brought Scott's turkey sandwich instead of her own with ham. Since the Thanksgiving dinner as a child when she got sick and threw up, Sarah had hated turkey and couldn't eat it. Just the smell alone made her feel sick. She texted Scott a picture of the sandwich, followed by an emoji laughing so hard it cried. Later, her boss yelled at her for placing the new bath towels from Huntley on the wrong shelf, and she had to excuse herself and say she didn't know where her head was.

Now that she was finally coming up her driveway and stopped the car in front of the small townhouse she shared with her boyfriend; she felt a sigh of great relief leave her body. Finally, she could relax. Nothing had worked out today, and there wasn't enough coffee in the world to make her feel better.

At least, now that she was home, she could get a glass of wine. She would put on some comfortable clothes and just relax—maybe binge some Netflix until Scott came home.

Sarah got out of the car and walked up toward the front door when she noticed something on the doorstep. The sight made her smile and forget all about the dreadful day, at least for a few seconds.

It was a huge bouquet of beautiful white lilies.

Her favorites.

She reached down and grabbed them, still smiling and shaking her head while mumbling, "Scott, you really shouldn't have."

She unlocked the door, holding the bouquet close to her chest, then walked into the kitchen and placed it on the granite counter-top. She put her purse down, then found the big clear glass vase on top of the fridge and poured water into it.

They had been dating for two years now and living together for the past six months. It was a rental, and Scott talked about finding

3

something they could buy together, but Sarah hesitated. She wanted to make sure they really meant it, that they could figure things out before making such a big decision.

Looking at the flowers, she suddenly realized she was in way deeper than she had thought. She was really in love with him.

She unpacked the lilies and looked for the card but didn't find any. Scott wasn't a man of big words, so it was no surprise, she thought and shrugged it off. He had probably decided to send her the flowers because he was sad about the sandwich mix-up today. Or maybe he just thought she needed it. Scott was a guy who would surprise her like that. He was the type who was always there at the right time and place.

"There, that looks great," she said as she let go of the flowers in the vase, and they folded out to show their splendor. The bouquet was even bigger than she had thought, and she wondered if it hadn't been too expensive.

Sarah took a picture of them, then sent a text to Scott:

YOU REALLY SHOULDN'T HAVE

It took a few minutes before he answered:

I DIDN'T

Sarah stared at the display of her phone, puzzled at his response. She then lifted her gaze and looked at the flowers, now with a concerned look. If they weren't from Scott, then who?

Who else in this world knew how much she loved white lilies?

S arah felt her hand holding the phone begin to shake. Then she put it down, grabbed the flowers, and threw them in the trash. She stood and stared at the trash bin for a few minutes, her heart throbbing in her throat. Then she realized she needed the flowers out of the house completely. The mere thought of having them inside made the hairs rise on the back of her neck.

She grabbed the garbage bag, closed it, carried it outside, and then threw it in the big bin. She slammed the lid shut. Sarah stared at it, almost feeling as if the flowers could jump out of it and attack her.

They're just flowers, Sarah.

Sarah took a couple of deep breaths to calm herself, then walked back to the porch. As she came in through the door, she stopped, sensing something. She turned and looked just in time to see a truck go by her house, driving very slowly.

Their house was at the end of a cul-de-sac. It wasn't often cars drove by if they didn't come to visit Sarah and Scott. Some people would accidentally come down their street, then use it to turn around, and that was all the traffic they usually got. Sarah stared at the pick-up truck as it continued past her house, still going very slowly. She tried to peek inside the cabin, but the windows were dark, and she couldn't see who was sitting in it. It returned to the street, then sped up while Sarah looked after it, heart pumping in her throat.

Easy now, Sarah.

Sarah watched as the truck disappeared completely, then turned around and went back inside, closing the door and locking it safely. She walked to the kitchen and poured herself a glass of white wine, her hand still shaking as she tipped the bottle. She sipped the drink, letting the wine run down her throat and do what it did best, calming her. Except it didn't really work. Her heart was still beating rapidly, and she had a hard time finding rest. She walked back and forth by the kitchen window, sipping her wine, staring out into the street.

You're paranoid, Sarah. It's impossible.

Sarah took another sip, then decided it was time to stop staring out the window. She was about to turn and walk away when she spotted the pick-up truck again. It was driving up the street once more and soon entering the cul-de-sac. It was going even slower this time like the driver was trying to figure out if this was the right place or not.

Sarah gasped lightly, then walked back into the living room, holding a hand on her chest and her beating heart. She sat down on the couch, then looked at the phone, wondering if she should text Scott. She knew he had a meeting with a potential new client today, one that he had worked on landing for months. Life as a freelance graphic designer could at times be tough, especially when the economy was suffering. Scott hadn't had many new clients this past year.

You can't disturb him now.

Sarah sighed and put the phone down, then closed her eyes briefly, once again reminding herself that it wasn't possible—that what she was imagining couldn't possibly be happening.

You're seeing things, making them up. You'll end up paranoid if you're not careful. You'll be one of Scott's clients.

She breathed again, easy and steadily, focusing on just that. Breathe in, hold it, and breathe out.

It worked. Her heart calmed, and as she opened her eyes again, she noticed something that immediately got her pulse to spike again, even worse than earlier.

There was something on top of the fireplace. Something she knew she hadn't put there.

"What in the…"

Sarah jumped up, then grabbed the frame between her hands. The picture inside it had been replaced with another one.

One from her past. A picture of her taken five years earlier in a different place and time.

Sarah clasped her mouth and could barely breathe as she stared at herself from years ago. She pulled out the picture and set it on fire before throwing it in the fireplace. The tears began to flow just as there was a knock on the door. She dropped the empty frame, then turned to look.

Out in the driveway, she saw the pick-up truck. It had parked behind her car, and whoever was in it was now by her door —wanting in.

Part I

ONE WEEK LATER

Cocoa Beach, Florida

I hid my face between my hands. I was sitting up in bed, looking down at Matt on the floor. He was kneeling while holding up the ring, an insecure smile on his lips. On my stomach slept Angelina— or *Angel* as we called her—our newborn. She was only three weeks old and still so small and fragile it seemed impossible she'd ever become as big as my other three children. I had just finished nursing her, and now she was sound asleep, acting like she hadn't awakened me every two hours all night.

"So, what do you say?" Matt asked, his voice shivering.

I stared down at him, then reached out my hand and touched his cheek. "I thought you'd never ask. Yes, I'll marry you, Matt."

He smiled, then rose to his feet and put the ring on my finger, or tried to, but my finger was still quite swollen from the extra pregnancy weight, and it didn't fit. This was disappointing to Matt. I could tell by the look on his face.

"Put it on the pinky instead," I said. "For now."

He did, and it barely fit, but I didn't care. I was just so happy finally to hear the words coming from his mouth. And to be honest, I couldn't have imagined a better or more romantic situation. Just the three of us together. The past weeks had been so intense, so incredibly wonderful; I could barely contain it—so much love, also between my older children and their little sister. The only one who seemed to struggle slightly with the newcomer was Matt's son, Elijah. I couldn't blame him. He had lost his mother and just recently connected with Matt as he came to live with him. It was easy for him to believe he might be forgotten with a newborn in the way.

We were all living in my small four-bedroom house, and my mom, who had lived with us until recently, had finally gotten herself a condo on the beach. I missed her since I had gotten used to having her around, but it was the right decision. We were a family now, and it was as it should be. Except Alex and Elijah had to share a room, and they weren't exactly excited about that. We had talked about finding something bigger, but I found it hard to leave my little home that I had gotten acquainted with after my ex-husband left me and later was killed.

It felt like home.

Plus, I wasn't sure we could even afford to buy something bigger with the upcoming wedding and everything.

Matt kissed me, and I felt tears run down my cheeks. I was so happy at this very moment; it seemed like a dream.

"I love you," I whispered. "It was always you; you know that, right?"

He nodded and placed his forehead gently against mine. "There was never anyone else for me."

I sniffled and wiped my eyes with my hand. I felt so extremely emotional these past few weeks, and I cried at even the smallest things. But today, it was okay to cry. I had waited for so long for Matt to pop the question, and finally, he had. Nothing could spoil this perfect moment—nothing.

"Mom?"

I looked up toward the doorway. "Christine? What are you doing home? School started two hours ago."

She hesitated in the doorway. I was about to tell her that Matt had proposed, but I sensed it wasn't the right time. Something was going on with her.

"What's up, sweetie?"

"I...I kind of need your help. And it kind of has to be quick. Now."

"Let me take Angel," Matt said and grabbed the baby. He held her tight to his body and walked to her crib, then put her down gently. Christine came closer, and I swung my legs out over the edge. She sat down next to me, and our eyes met.

"It's Amy," she said, her big eyes tearing up when talking about her friend. "I don't know what to do."

Chapter 1

THEN:

"I just don't understand why he doesn't hug me when I cry—when that is all I need from him."

Lynn Parks looked up at the woman, Joanna Harry, on the couch in front of her. Next to her sat her boyfriend, Jeffrey Johnson, in his two-thousand-dollar pinstriped suit. They had held hands on their first visits to Lynn's office. They had been coming for three months, and now, they weren't holding hands anymore.

Lynn wrote on her notepad, then lifted her gaze to meet Jeff's again. "And what do you say to that, Jeff? Why do you think that is?"

He threw out his hands. "I don't know. I mean, she's…sometimes she seems like she wants me to leave her alone when she's upset. Maybe she could tell me when she wants me to hug her and when she doesn't because I don't know."

Lynn nodded. Her eyes stayed locked with Jeff's for a few seconds longer, just to make sure he didn't have anything else to add. Then, she looked at Joanna. "Is that something you might be able to do? Tell Jeff when you need him to affirm you and when he doesn't? Sort of guiding him along the way?"

Joanna sighed and rolled her eyes. "But shouldn't he know these things by now?"

Lynn closed her eyes briefly and hoped they didn't see. It wasn't her job to judge, but she often felt that Joanna demanded a lot from Jeff.

"We've been dating less than a year," Jeff said. He had a little smirk on his lip that always made Lynn smile. His blue eyes lingered on her a lot during their conversations, and they had come to learn during their sessions that it was a pattern in his life—flirting with women to feel superior to them. It was one of the reasons his girlfriend had wanted them to seek counseling. They were planning on marrying within the next year, but she wanted to make sure they were suitable and hopefully have him stop looking at other women. That's how she had put it during their first session. She wanted them to be close, but Jeff wasn't doing enough.

"I'm trying my best here," he added and leaned back on the couch, stretching out his arms behind his girlfriend, struggling to kill the smirk.

"Trying your best?" she squealed. "It sure doesn't feel like it. Last weekend at the bar, you were flirting with that woman, remember? The blonde one?"

"I was just talking to her. Her boyfriend was right there next to her. I wasn't flirting at all."

Joanna's shoulders slumped, and she turned away from him. "You see what I have to put up with here? I don't want to end up like some suburban housewife who doesn't know where her husband is or who he is doing."

"At some point, you'll just have to trust him, Joanna," Lynn said. "We all have to trust the ones we choose to marry."

"Yeah, you totally have trust issues," Jeff said, leaning forward.

Lynn didn't know much about him except that he was an investment banker and made a lot of money. She couldn't blame Joanna for being nervous since he was a very handsome guy, tall and blond with the bluest eyes Lynn had ever seen.

Lynn looked at the clock on the wall next to her. She had let them go over time without noticing it.

"I'm afraid our time is up for today. Let's continue where we left off next time, okay?"

They got up, and Joanna rushed toward the door, while Jeff didn't seem to be in any hurry to get out. He smiled at Lynn as he passed her, then winked.

"See you next week, Doc."

She closed the door before he could notice that she blushed.

Chapter 2

"Y ou mean to tell me that Amy has been here the entire time?"

I knelt next to the girl on the floor in the bathroom. The house Christine had taken me to was for sale and abandoned. I pushed away a dead roach lying on its back.

Christine nodded. "Her parents wanted her to get rid of the baby, but she didn't. So, we brought her here, and she's been living here the past several months. I've been bringing her food and whatever else she needed. But last night she…she started to feel pain, and when I came to see her this morning on my way to school, as usual, she was screaming."

Amy was sweating and let out a loud groan as another contraction waved through her body.

"Her water broke like half an hour ago, and that's when I thought I'd come to get you," Christine said. "I don't know what to do."

I stared at the young girl, no more than fifteen. Christine had told me that Amy had gotten pregnant a long time ago, but I had assumed that she had an abortion since I didn't hear anything else. I knew that was what her parents wanted. I couldn't believe she had been hiding in this house for months, and Christine had kept this a secret from me.

"What the heck, Christine?" I said. "What was your plan? To have her give birth here? In all this dirt?"

"I…I don't know," she said, half crying. "I don't think…I mean, we…"

Amy let out another loud groan, and I realized she was closer than I had thought. I had to act fast.

"We need to get an ambulance," I said and grabbed my phone. I looked at Christine. "I'll deal with you later."

The ambulance came quickly, but by then, it was too late to move her. The EMTs decided they had to let her have the baby there, and Christine held Amy's hands as she went into labor right there on the bathroom floor of an abandoned house.

"There you go, Amy. You've got this," I squealed and remembered my own birth just a few weeks earlier. It had gone pretty smoothly and uneventful since it was my fourth child. Amy's was painful; I could tell, and I truly felt for her. My first birth to Olivia sixteen years ago had lasted thirty-six hours, and even though I did get an epidural, I still felt the pain in a way that made me force Chad to promise me we'd never have any more children. A year later, I had forgotten everything about the pain, clever as the body is, to be able to block out that sort of thing entirely, and we tried again, making Christine.

"That's it," the female EMT said. "Push, Amy. Push."

Amy did, and I watched as the head came first, and then a few seconds later, the EMT was able to pull the baby out with the joyful squeal: "It's a boy!"

That's when I broke down in tears for the second time today. The miracle of birth was unlike anything in this world.

"Can I see him?" Amy said, sobbing with happiness. The EMT handed him to her, and her body trembled as she looked down at his beautiful, wrinkled face. Now, we were all crying, even Christine, who simply couldn't hold it back. I grabbed her and hugged her tightly while we cried together, Christine still holding Amy's hand in hers.

"He's so beautiful," Amy said. "He's the most beautiful thing I have ever seen."

"He sure is," I said.

"But now, we need to get you both to the hospital," the EMT said.

Amy's eyes grew wide and big. "But…I don't…I don't have any insurance."

"What about your parents?" I asked.

She shook her head. "They won't…they threw me out."

That brought a different type of tears to my eyes. I grabbed her by the shoulders and made sure she looked at me while I spoke, "I'll take care of it. Don't worry, sweetie. You're not alone. We've got you."

Chapter 3

He saw them from the car as they arrived. He held his breath as they passed him on his street, hurrying toward his townhouse at the end of the cul-de-sac. He watched in the rearview mirror as the three police cruisers parked in his driveway, and seconds later, three officers stormed up on his porch.

Luckily, Scott had a feeling they were coming. He got into his car, then drove down to the end of the road just as they turned the corner of his street. Now, he was at the end of the street; he then took a quick right turn before stepping on it, accelerating down the main road, hoping and praying they didn't have any of their colleagues on traffic patrol nearby.

Scott felt the sweat tickle his upper lip and wiped it off. This had been a little too close for comfort. He wondered where he could go as he reached the city limits and sped up.

Heart in his throat, he took off toward a friend's house, then walked up and knocked on the door. Aiden opened the door, then shook his head at him.

"What are you doing here, Scott?" he asked, closing the door behind him and walking out on the porch. His voice was almost a whisper. "You shouldn't be here. Lisa will kill me if she finds out you're here."

"I didn't know where else to go," Scott said, keeping his voice low. "The police came to my house. I barely made it out."

"They're looking for you everywhere. They even came here and asked all these questions about you and your relationship with Sarah. It got Lisa all worked up. *I always knew there was something bad about him, Aiden. Scott has always given me these bad vibes;* she kept saying to me. She made me promise that I'd never see you again. You know they think you might have killed Sarah, right?"

Scott swallowed. He suddenly felt so weary.

"I just need somewhere to crash for the night. I'll be gone in the morning. I can sleep in the garage on that old couch you keep in there. You won't even know I'm there."

Aiden gave him a look, then ran a hand frantically through his hair. "You know I would...if it wasn't for Lisa. I...I'm sorry, old friend. I can't...she'll kill me, or even worse, leave me."

Scott stared at Aiden. They had known each other since college. Was it really so easy to throw away a friendship like this?

"I didn't do it," Scott said. "You have to believe me."

Aiden hesitated. The pause was a little too long for comfort and told Scott exactly how he felt.

"You gotta be kidding me," Scott said and took a step back. "You don't even believe me, do you?"

Aiden threw out his arms resignedly. "I...I don't know what to think, to be honest, Scott. I'm trying to stay out of it and not pick a side here."

Scott nodded and clicked his tongue. "Well, I guess you just did anyway. It's good to know who your real friends are."

He turned around and walked down the steps to the front yard toward the car. Aiden yelled after him, "Scott, don't be like that..."

Scott didn't pay any more attention to his old friend. He backed out of the driveway, then grabbed his phone as he drove down the street and called his parents.

"You know, Scott, we would have you any time, but tonight is not a good night," his dad said when he asked if he could crash in their guest room. "Your mom isn't feeling well, and you know how she gets."

Scott sighed deeply and guessed that the police had been at their door as well, then he hung up. He drove out I95 and went north; when he saw the exit sign to Cocoa Beach, he made a sharp turn, driving onto the ramp.

Chapter 4

I stayed with Christine at the hospital to make sure Amy and the baby were both okay. She was smiling, but I believed I saw a deep hurt underneath. I grabbed my phone and called her parents. I had known Phil and Kim Robinson for some time now since our daughters were good friends. They seemed like good people to me. They needed to know that they were now grandparents. Seeing that adorable little baby would have to make them feel differently about the situation.

Who wouldn't go completely soft when seeing him?

No one picked up, and I tried again but still got only Kim's voice mail. I decided not to leave a message since something like this had to be handled delicately.

It was best if it was delivered in person.

I walked back into the room, then kissed Amy on the forehead. "I have to get back to Angel, but Christine will stay here, right, sweetie?"

Christine nodded. "I'll stay. I'm not going anywhere."

I smiled, feeling proud of my daughter and her compassion for her friend. I wasn't angry anymore that she had kept it a secret. I now realized she was just doing what she believed was best for her friend and because this was how Amy wanted it. They were teenagers. They didn't think of consequences.

"All right. See you in a few hours, then," I said. "Call or text if you need me."

Christine hugged me. "Thank you, Mom."

I closed my eyes and enjoyed her embrace. At that age, you never knew when you'd get one again. "You're welcome, sweetie. We all need to take care of one another."

I hurried to the elevator and into the parking lot. I got into my car, then drove down A1A, wondering about poor Amy and what her future would be. Surely, her parents would want to help her out the best they could. That was what we were there for, right? If it were me, I'd take the kid in and have her drop out of school, then retake this year next year while I cared for the child. Of course, not all parents had the privilege of working from home as I did, but I knew that Kim didn't work outside the home. Phil was the bread earner, and Kim had devoted her life to taking care of Amy, driving her to soccer, and making sure the snacks they brought were gluten-free. I knew it wasn't easy for her, but at some point, she'd have to accept that it happened and step up to help.

Right?

I parked in front of their two-story luxury house with river views from all sides, then got out. I hurried to the door with the palm trees carved into the glass and rang the doorbell.

It took a while for Kim to answer.

"Eva Rae?" she said with a stiff smile.

"I tried to call. Amy went into labor."

Kim shook her head. "I don't know what you're talking about."

"She had the baby, Kim. She's in the hospital."

Kim's eyes met mine, and I could see the terror in them. Her nostrils were flaring lightly as she was searching for what to say to me.

"It's a boy," I added. "A healthy baby boy. Your grandson."

Kim was just standing there in her purple and gray yoga outfit. She lifted her nose toward the sky and spoke in almost a whisper, "Please. Just leave."

"Kim," I said. I felt urgent desperation as it rushed through my veins. This couldn't be right. She couldn't have heard me right. "It's your daughter. She had a child. She needs her parents more than anything right now."

"I don't have a daughter anymore. Just leave. Please."

And just like that, she slammed the door shut in my face. I stood back, staring at the palm trees cut into it, suppressing my desire to kick down the door, grab her by the neck, and drag her with me to the hospital, or at least shake some sense into her.

How could anyone be this cruel?

I knew the feeling of rejection a little too well from my own mother when I was Amy's age, and I think that is why it angered me so much and why I made the decision I did.

Chapter 5

Then:
"You're alone today?"

Lynn looked at Jeffrey questioningly. He sat down on the couch, his hands folded in his lap. He seemed like a completely changed man, so different from the cocky guy with the handsome smirk she had gotten used to. He was still in an expensive suit, but it couldn't hide the fact that he seemed like a broken man. Lynn felt worried and sat up straight in her chair.

"Where is Joanna?"

His eyes didn't meet hers yet. They stared at his shoes, and his fingers fiddled with the edge of his suit jacket.

"Jeffrey?"

Finally, he lifted his gaze and looked into her eyes. Her heart sank when seeing the hurt in them.

"What happened? Can you tell me about it? Take your time if you have to. Settle down."

He sighed and fought his tears. The sight made Lynn feel so incredibly worried for him. This was a completely different Jeffrey than she had ever seen during their sessions. And if she was honest with herself, it woke some strong maternal feelings inside her. She felt an urge to protect him, to care for him.

"She left me," he said with a sniffle. "I'm sorry."

He reached for the box of Kleenex on the small table between them, then used one to wipe his eyes.

"Why do you say you're sorry?" Lynn asked.

He scoffed. "You must think I'm a total mess. It's not like I'm the first guy to be dumped in the world, right?"

Lynn couldn't take her eyes off of Jeffrey. Somehow, seeing his vulnerability had triggered something inside her, something profound that she struggled to understand. Gone was the alpha-male, the grin, and the constant flirt, but it didn't make him less attractive. Not by any means.

"You're right about that, but that doesn't mean it doesn't hurt. Let's help you work through this. Tell me what happened," Lynn said. "When did she leave you?"

Jeffrey moaned lightly. He was shifting in his seat. "The day after we were here last time. We had a huge fight when we got home, and then she packed her bags and left. She said she went to her mother's place, but I called there later when she wasn't picking up her phone, and her mom said she wasn't there. I haven't spoken to her since that day. I keep calling her, but she doesn't pick up. It's driving me nuts."

"Okay," Lynn said. "So, you think she might be with another man?"

Jeffrey's head jolted upright, and he stared at her. "Why? Do *you* think she is?"

Lynn took a deep breath.

His head slumped. "Of course not. You have no way of knowing that. I just… I always suspected that she might be seeing someone else."

"So, there's a jealousy matter there," Lynn said, squinting her eyes at him. "Is that something you'd like to work on? In our future sessions?"

Jeffrey glared at her. "You mean that? I can come back even if she's not with me?"

"Absolutely."

He sighed and leaned back, a look of relief on his face.

"Thank you, Doc. You have no clue how much that means to me. I felt like I was going to die this past week. I know I can talk to you. I feel like we have a real trust-thing going on here."

That made Lynn smile secretively. She felt that too, and she also felt that Jeffrey could be a good patient to work with, work through this break-up, while secretly suppressing that gnawing feeling inside of her that her motives for taking him on weren't as honorable as she made them out to be.

Chapter 6

"I'm giving Amy and the baby your room. So, you and Olivia will have to share a room from now on," I said as I drove up into the driveway and killed the engine. "Olivia agreed to it if I promised to get her a new computer, so she shouldn't give either of you a hard time."

A car I didn't know was parked on the street outside my front yard, and I glared at it as I got out, wondering if Olivia had company. I slammed the car door shut, then went to the back to help Amy out with the baby in her arms. She had been in the hospital for two days and was ready to go home, which was now in my house.

I held the door for Amy while she got out and carefully, holding the baby tightly, walked up to the house. Olivia came to the door as we walked up and held it open for us. I smiled at her and our eyes locked for a second. She grabbed me by the arm as I walked in.

"Someone is here to see you."

I lifted my eyebrows. "Who?"

She shrugged, annoyed. "How am I supposed to know? He's in the kitchen talking to Matt."

"Christine, can you show Amy to her room?" I asked. "Olivia, you help them too."

Olivia smiled and looked at the baby in Amy's arms. "Oh, my God. He's so tiny. And cute."

"Don't get any ideas," I said to her.

She stuck her tongue out at me when Alex, my seven-year-old son, came tumbling down the stairs.

"Mo-o-o-om, Mo-o-om!"

He ran toward me and bumped into my stomach head-first like a bull.

"See," I said. "This is what they turn into eventually."

I grabbed him and lifted him, even though he was a little too heavy for me. Then, I kissed his nose.

"What's up, buddy?"

He leaned his head on my chest. "I just missed you, is all."

I held him tight.

"Do you have a name for him yet?" Olivia asked Amy as they walked to the stairs. I had been busy the past two days, rearranging Christine's room into a nursery. I was pretty proud of my accomplishments and running on only a few hours of sleep since Angel kept waking me up every two hours. But I had experience enough to know it was only temporary.

"I was thinking about Owen," I heard Amy answer on her way up. I smiled, feeling pretty good about myself for helping her out this way, even though I knew it would be tight in our little house. Matt was very skeptical still, but I was hoping to get him onboard eventually. The last thing I wanted was for Amy to end up in some foster care and risk being separated from her baby. I couldn't live with myself if anything like that happened. I had assisted at her birth, which gave me some sort of attachment that I couldn't just let go of. You could say I felt responsible for the girl. After all, we were supposed to help out where we could. That had always been my mantra in life. Yes, it meant the girls had to squeeze together and that there would be two crying babies in the house instead of just the one, but so what? If anyone could do it, it was us.

I heard Angel cry, then walked into the kitchen where Matt was sitting with her, holding her on his arm, trying to feed her the bottle. The sight made my knees soft.

"There she is," Matt said.

I turned to look at who he was talking to. My smile stiffened as I laid eyes upon him, and suddenly all I wanted to do was turn around and run.

Chapter 7

"S-Scott?"

I put down my purse, my heart racing in my chest. I could barely look at the man. He was so handsome, sitting there on the stool, a cup of coffee in front of him. I was suddenly very aware that I hadn't showered in two days and was wearing no make-up. My hair was up in a ponytail, so you couldn't see how greasy it was. I was wearing sweatpants and a T-shirt I hadn't even looked at before putting it on this morning in the darkness, afraid I might wake up Angel, who finally fell asleep around seven when I had to get the older kids ready for school.

He smiled. I had forgotten that teeth could be so straight and pearly white. Didn't this man age or drink coffee that would stain his teeth?

It wasn't fair.

A few strands of gray on the sides of his head told me he had, after all, aged, but they looked good on him, a little too good.

"Eva Rae."

He got up, opened his arms, and pulled me into a deep hug.

"Okay, we're doing that now," I mumbled as I felt his arms around me. I blushed and tried to avoid his eyes as he let go of me.

"How have you been?" he asked, trying to catch my eye. "It's been ages."

I lifted my gaze, and our eyes locked, even though I tried not to. "You look great. Really great."

Again, I blushed, and I worried Matt would see it, so I looked at him instead and then at our beautiful baby.

"Thanks, I am great, actually. Life is good."

"Sure looks like it. You got the house full. Lucky you. And you and Matt are a couple now, huh? That's amazing."

I nodded, my eyes still avoiding his. I reached out my hands to take Angel, and Matt gave her to me. Feeling her close to my chest again made me calmer. She was dozing off in my arms.

"So… Scott? What brings you here?" I asked, puzzled. Being in his presence made me nervous, and I kind of felt like I was a teenager again. It wasn't a comfortable feeling, that's for sure.

Scott's expression changed to a serious one. He sat back down. "As I was just telling Matt, I've come because I'm in trouble."

I rocked Angel from side to side, looking down at her beautiful face, then back up at Scott.

"What kind of trouble?"

"Maybe I should take Angel upstairs," Matt said and got up. "She's asleep."

I looked down at my gorgeous child, then sighed. He was right. She needed to be somewhere quiet. I was just disappointed since I had been looking forward to holding her again. I handed her to Matt, who smiled at the sight of his daughter. He looked so sexy with our baby on his arm.

"I'll get her to bed."

I exhaled and sat down, yet felt strangely at unease as Matt left me alone with Scott.

Scott's green eyes lingered on me, and I saw almost despair in them. They were begging me, as he said, "The kind of trouble only a former FBI-profiler can help me out of."

Chapter 8

"You're telling me you're on the run from the police right now?"
I stared at Scott, and he grimaced.

"It's bad, isn't it?"

"Yeah, it's bad. It's awful. Did you tell Matt? You know he's CBPD, right?"

He nodded. "I know. I know. I just didn't know where else to go. Then I remembered that I read recently that you moved back and that you solved that Nancy Henry case, and I was so impressed since it was really complicated. I was on I95 and had decided to run when I saw the exit sign to Cocoa Beach and thought of you. Only you can help me. I am innocent, Eva Rae. I haven't hurt her."

I stared at him, then sipped the coffee I had poured myself while Scott told me everything.

"And you say she just disappeared? Any signs of forced entry?"

He shook his head. "All I found was an empty picture frame on the living room floor. Nothing else."

I gave him a look. I saw the desperation in his eyes. It was hard to miss.

"Well, I have known you for years, Scott, and even though you acted like a prick back in the day, I don't believe you would harm anyone."

"Thank you," he said, relieved. "You're the first to say so. All my friends, even my parents, don't want to have anything to do with me. They think I did it, that I did something to her. Can you believe them?"

I sipped my coffee pensively. "Could she have left you? Is there a reason why no one thinks that's a possibility?"

"I think she'd at least say goodbye," he said. "Or leave a note."

"When was the last time you heard from her? Was it when you said goodbye in the morning, or did you talk during the day?"

"She texted me because she had received flowers, and she thought they were from me. But I told her that I hadn't sent any. When I came home, they were in the trash bin outside."

That made me frown.

"Flowers?"

"Yes, lilies. They were her favorites, and so she immediately thought they were from me."

"But you didn't send any. Could it have been someone else she knows? Her parents?"

"She didn't speak to her parents. I never met them, and she didn't like to talk about them."

"Hm, why not?"

He shrugged. "She never told me."

"Did you ask?"

He smiled. "I know you think I'm a cold bastard, but people change, Eva Rae. Yes, of course, I asked. She didn't want to tell me. She had moved far away from them because she didn't want to see them. She came down here from Ohio and wanted to start over."

"Was she generally very secretive about her past? Like did she have friends from before she moved down here? Did anyone visit with you?"

He shook his head. "None. She never spoke of anyone from her past."

I paused, then thought of my baby upstairs. "I don't know, Scott…"

His eyes were begging. He put a hand on top of mine, and I froze. His touch brought me back to years ago. My heart was pounding at the memory.

Careful, Eva Rae.

"Please. Eva Rae. I have nowhere else to turn."

I exhaled. "I just had a baby, Scott. Things are kind of tight and messy around here right now. I wouldn't even know where to begin. For all I know, Sarah just left you, and maybe she went back to some guy she hadn't told you about. Besides, if the police can't prove you hurt her, then they can't charge you with anything. I suggest you get a good lawyer instead. I can help you with that."

"I don't think that is what happened," Scott said. "She didn't just leave. Or I wouldn't be here."

I rubbed my eyes. Exhaustion was beginning to set in. This was so not what I needed right now.

"I'm sorry, Scott... I can't..."

He grabbed my arm and forced me to look at him. The deep desperation in his eyes got to me.

"I'm telling you—something happened to her. I know it did."

"And how do you know?"

He sighed. "Because she told me two months ago that if she ever went missing, I should look for her."

Chapter 9

THEN:

"How have you been? You seem a little...quiet today?"

Lynn sent Jeffrey a compassionate smile. He looked great, as usual, impeccably dressed in his pinstriped suit and white shirt underneath. His expensive watch dangled from his wrist, but there was something different about him—a sadness she hadn't seen in him before. He had arrived a few minutes late for their appointment and had barely looked at her.

"Is something wrong?" she added after a few seconds of silence.

She couldn't help smiling when she looked at him. She couldn't tell him, but she had been looking forward to their session all weekend. She had thought about him a lot, maybe even more than she should have. She couldn't help it. There was something about him that made her care for him. She had wondered if it was a maternal instinct that had awoken in her. Did she care for him the way a mother would a child?

"Jeffrey?"

He looked up. Were those tears in his eyes?

"It's just... well, I miss her so much."

Lynn exhaled. "You mean Joanna?"

He nodded. "She was the one for me, you know?"

"Okay. Let's talk about that."

Lynn straightened in her chair.

"I don't know," he said. "What's there to talk about?"

"I have a feeling there's more than you think. Have you seen her recently?"

"I see her...from time to time."

Lynn looked at him from above her reading glasses. "You see her? Where?"

He shrugged and looked away. His eyes hit the bookshelves to his right. There was something he wasn't telling her.

"Just...around."

Lynn tilted her head slightly. "Okay, just so I understand better, you see her around, you say, but could you tell me where you see her? At the supermarket?"

"Among other places...yes."

"At her house?"

"Maybe."

Lynn swallowed, then took off her glasses and looked at him. "Have you been following her?"

His eyes hit the floor. He shrugged. "Maybe...a little."

She sighed and closed her eyes briefly. She wasn't supposed to pass judgment, so she'd have to be careful how she said the next thing.

"Does that sound like a good idea?"

He shrugged again. "I don't know. It's not something I plan to do. It just happens. I drive past her house and see her come out the door, and then I follow her. I just feel...it's hard to live without her. You must know this. You know with your sister and all."

Lynn swallowed again, then wrinkled her forehead.

"My sister?"

"Yes, how she fell in love with a guy and then killed herself because he dumped her."

Lynn's heart stopped. "That's not exactly what happened, but that's not important. How do you know this?"

He lifted his gaze, and his eyes met hers. "From Facebook. You wrote a post about it on the fifth anniversary of it happening. It was really sad to read."

Lynn put the pen down. A strange sensation rushed through her body, which she pushed away as fast as possible.

"You've been checking my Facebook account?"

He blushed. "No, no…I mean, yes…I did…but just once."

"That is not a very good idea, Jeffrey," she said. "And I think you know it. You and I have a different kind of relationship. We're not friends. I am your therapist."

He looked sheepishly at her. "O-of course. I didn't mean anything by it. I just…I was curious. I won't do it again. I promise."

His gaze made her smile. She couldn't help herself; she felt flattered. He wasn't the first patient to have checked her social media profiles or Google her name. One had even run a background check on her, getting her address and phone number. It wasn't unusual to be curious like Jeffrey said. Most patients were. But she knew it was essential to stop that sort of behavior right away. Patients were supposed to become attached to their therapists, but there had to be clear boundaries from the beginning. Once one of them overstepped those boundaries, the relationship would shift, and it would become something other than a patient-therapist relationship.

And that was where the danger lay.

Chapter 10

Matt stood with his arms crossed while I finished my breakfast. Angel was napping in her crib upstairs, and I was hurrying to be done with my food so I could get dressed. All the kids had left for school—except Amy and Owen, of course—and the house had finally gone calm.

"You actually told him you'd help him?" he asked, giving me one of his angry and disapproving looks. "You want to help that prick?"

I looked up at him. "That's not very nice."

"But that's what he was back then. We hated him, remember?"

"That was twenty years ago, Matt. He is in trouble now. Something happened to his girlfriend. I can't just not help him because we didn't like him back in high school."

He lifted his eyebrows. "I just don't get it. What is it with you two, anyway? I didn't even know you knew one another. You barely spoke back then."

I sipped my coffee and closed my eyes briefly. I really didn't want to get into it now. I wasn't sure I ever wanted to. It had stirred up some strong emotions from back then that I didn't really want to resurface. But I just couldn't get that sentence out of my mind again. His girlfriend had known something might happen to her. She had warned him.

"We don't know one another very well," I said. "I just want to help him, okay? It's not so much for his sake as it is for his girlfriend's. If she told him that he should look for her if she ever disappeared, then she must have feared that something would happen to her. I can't stop thinking about her."

"And what about Angel?" he asked. "Who's gonna take care of her? I have to go to work."

"I'll bring her with me," I said with a shrug. "As soon as she wakes up and I've changed her and fed her, I'll go."

He tilted his head. "And you're sure that's a good idea?"

I scoffed. "It's not like I'm going somewhere dangerous. I'm just going to talk to the detective on the case. He's an old colleague of mine, and he owes me a favor."

Matt smiled and shook his head. "You're incredible; do you know that?"

"I hope that is meant as a compliment," I said and sipped more coffee. I was going to need it to stay focused today. Angel had kept me awake from two until four o'clock, refusing to fall asleep. I had ended up sleeping with her while sitting in my chair, the baby lying on my chest. That was how we woke up this morning.

Matt grabbed a bowl and poured in some cereal, then started to eat. "I don't understand why you can't stay home and enjoy this time with Angel?"

I sighed. "Just let me have this, okay? I'm going a little stir-crazy home alone all day. Helping Scott and maybe Sarah out will give me something to do. A purpose."

"And taking care of our baby isn't purpose enough?" he asked, crunching his cereal loudly.

I finished my cup and put it down. "Let it go, will you?"

I rose to my feet, then leaned over and kissed his milky lips before Angel's crying stopped us.

"I just wish you'd tell me why you two seem to know each other so well," he said as I ran up the stairs to attend to her. "You're being weird about it."

I stopped briefly at the top of the stairs, biting my lip, thinking back on Scott and what had happened back then, then sighed. Angel's insistent cries pulled me back to reality, and I rushed into her nursery and smiled as I saw her beautiful face staring back at me from inside the crib. It was amazing how one small smile from such a little creature could make all my problems and bad thoughts disappear in a heartbeat. I grabbed her in my arms, then heard the front door slam shut as Matt left for work.

Chapter 11

"Eva Rae Thomas!"

I opened the door to Detective Jake Perez's office at Rockledge Police Department. He was part of the Criminal Investigations Division, and he was the lead investigator on the case of the missing Sarah Abbey. I had worked another case with him ten years ago, back when he was in Tallahassee, and I had saved his life in a shootout with a serial killer who strangled his victims as part of a sexual ritual.

Jake looked at Angel, who was strapped to my chest in her sling.

"Cute kid. I can't believe you're still having more?"

I sat down in a chair across from him, ignoring his comment that obviously revealed that he thought I was a little old for having a baby.

"What can I do for you?" he asked. "You said on the phone that it was about the Sarah Abbey case? What's your interest in that?"

"It's a long story," I said, looking down briefly at the baby as she started to complain. I found the pacifier and tried to get her to take it, but she hadn't really accepted it yet and spat it out as soon as I tried.

"I have a lot of time," Jake said.

"I just want to ask you for some details, if I may," I said.

He leaned back in his chair and crossed his arms. "I'm not really allowed to since you're technically not working. You quit, right?"

"Yeah, well, that didn't really work. Work has sort of kept following me since I stopped. But technically, no, I'm not FBI anymore."

He bit the inside of his cheek, then shook his head. "I don't think I can help you, Eva Rae; I'm sorry."

Angel fussed, and I tried the pacifier once more. It stuck for about a second before she spat it right out again. I couldn't figure out why she wouldn't take it. All my other children had loved their pacifiers from the first moment I introduced them.

"Come on, Jake. I just need to take a look."

He gave me a glare across the room, then tilted his head while rubbing his stubble. "Oh, I have a feeling I'm going to regret this big time."

I smiled. "You're the best, Jake."

He pointed at me. "But that means we're even."

I gaped. "What? I saved your life. No way does that make us even."

He rolled his office chair to the file cabinet, then flipped through the dividers and pulled one out. He threw it on the desk in front of me.

"I'm going for coffee. You have ten minutes."

"That's all I need," I said.

He walked out while I opened the file, trying to calm Angel, but she was getting annoyed now and wouldn't keep quiet. I flipped through the pages, reading the details when I came to something that made me pause and reread it just to be sure. I stared at the page for a few seconds, pondering the information, then continued. By the time Jake came back, I was done and rose to my feet.

"You leaving so soon?" he said, holding two cups of coffee in his hands. I smiled at his sweet gesture. Angel was not just fussing now but starting to cry. "As much as I would love to stay and catch up on old times, I have to get this one home and feed her before she gets really upset," I said and rushed out the door, feeling satisfied that I had gotten what I came for, and then some.

Chapter 12

He was sitting in the corner of Juice 'N Java, a local coffee shop in Cocoa Beach. Lily Mitchell spotted him from behind the counter and smiled as she took the customer's credit card and swiped it. It had been like this all morning. He would sit there, stare at her, and their eyes would meet. She smiled back, showing him what her boyfriend referred to as her *charming overbite*.

The customer got his coffee and bagel, then left. Lily remained at the cash register for a few seconds, fixing the receipts, then lifted her gaze again and met his. He smiled, and she smiled back, then lowered her eyes shyly.

She wasn't sure why he was watching her so intently. He was handsome yet significantly older than her. Did he think she would be interested in someone like him?

The guy sipped more coffee when the door opened, and two local police officers stepped in. Lily studied the guy as his eyes grew wide, and he turned away.

The officers walked up to Lily and ordered their usual sandwiches. Lily noticed how the panic was painted all over the guy's face as they looked around them, waiting for their coffee. He grabbed a magazine that was just lying there and looked through it, lowering his head as much as possible.

What's he doing?

The officers received their coffee and breakfast in a bag, then thanked Lily, and one of them put a tip in the jar with a wink. They turned around and started to head for the door. The guy in the corner lowered his eyes and looked into the magazine. He was sweating heavily, and his torso was shaking. It seemed very suspicious, and for a second, Lily wondered if she should tell the officers. This guy had been acting strangely ever since he got here and ordered coffee from her, unable to take his eyes off of her. And now this? The officers walked toward the door when one of them stopped and turned to look.

He's looking straight at him.

Lily held her breath while the officer stared at him. Neither of them moved a muscle.

Why is he just standing there?

Lily's stomach turned to knots, and it felt like an eternity went by before the officer's radio scratched, and he grabbed it, then spoke into it, running out the door, forgetting all about the guy in the corner.

Lily breathed. Maybe he wasn't some wanted criminal after all. Perhaps he was just actually reading that magazine. The guy didn't look up until the police cruiser drove past the window of the coffee shop. Lily stared at him while he breathed heavily, then finally was able to calm himself down just enough to finish his coffee.

Something is seriously off with this guy.

It was the end of Lily's shift, so she took off her apron, then walked into the back and came out with her purse in hand. She walked toward her car when she spotted the guy from the coffee house walking out as well, his eyes still lingering on her. She paused for a second and looked at him, then felt a chill run down her spine. She turned around and rushed toward her car. She started the engine, then drove onto A1A, looking anxiously in the mirror to see if his car followed her.

Chapter 13

THEN:

"What's up with you today? You've barely said a word since you got here."

Lynn corrected her shirt. She had worn one that showed a little cleavage today, but now, she regretted it. She didn't usually wear shirts like this. She knew why she had done it, and it made her feel silly. She should know better than to dress up for a patient. She even wore make-up. She never usually wore more than just a little mascara.

Jeffrey rubbed his hands together. He didn't look at her, but she could tell something was tormenting him.

"It's just…well…"

"Take your time," she said, "to find the words."

He sighed, then finally lifted his eyes to meet hers. "It's just that…well, I can't stop thinking about you. I know I'm not supposed to, but I can't help myself. I look forward to our sessions so much."

She felt a deep warmth rush through her body as the words fell. Her heart started to beat faster, and she felt such deep love for him in that instant.

"That's okay," she said, looking down briefly at her notepad.

"It's normal to get attached to your therapist. It's actually what's supposed to happen. It shows the therapy is working."

His eyes grew wider, and his face lit up. "So, you're not mad at me?"

That made her smile softly. "Of course not. Therapy is an intimate setting, and the relationship is quite special. But it must remain in this room, and there can be no physical contact."

Lynn exhaled deeply. She was doing the right thing; setting the boundaries was so crucial at this stage.

"I just…I have this deep fear that I will lose you," he said. "It's driving me crazy."

She smiled again and tilted her head. "That's perfectly normal too. You have some serious abandonment issues that you're trying to work your way through. Your girlfriend left you, and now you're transferring those emotions and fears onto me. But rest assured, I am not going anywhere."

Lynn tried hard to suppress her blushing, but with no luck. She felt her cheeks grow warm. It was such a sweet moment for them both. Jeffrey was getting attached to her. It was only natural, but a part of her couldn't help enjoying it. It was sweet and made him so vulnerable.

"It just…it hurts," he said and put a hand on his chest. "I don't like depending on anyone. It makes me feel needy—like I was with her."

"We're talking about Joanna now, right? Do you still see her?

He blushed.

"Jeffrey, we talked about this. Stalking her isn't doing either of you any good. You need to let her go."

He nodded. "I know. I know. It's just…I'm so angry at her for leaving me. I can't stand it. No one leaves me. It hurt so much, and it makes me obsessed with getting her back, and…"

"Controlling her?" Lynn asked. "Do you think that's why you're following her?"

He looked up and nodded. "Yeah, that's probably it. You're good, Doc; do you know that? You're really good."

She blushed again, cursing herself for not being able to hide her own emotions better.

"I do my best."

"I mean, that is totally what I have been thinking, that I want to control her. I mean, I even fantasized about locking her up in my basement, heh."

Lynn looked up from her notepad. "Excuse me?"

He shook his head. "No, no, don't take it the wrong way. I just fantasized about it; that's all. Like people have fantasies, you know, but now that you've explained it to me, it makes complete sense. I just want to control her, and I need to stop that. It's not so much her I want as it is the fact that I can't stand that she is the one who left me. I have never been left before, Doc. It's not easy for me."

Lynn swallowed hard. She looked into Jeffrey's eyes to be sure he was telling her the truth. He smiled softly, and that melted her heart. Then she nodded.

"I think you're reaching new levels of understanding here, Jeffrey. Good work today."

Chapter 14

"Scott, when you hear this, please call me back. I need to talk to you."

I left the second message while Alex pulled my arm.

"Mom, Mom, listen to me!"

I hung up, then glared down at him. In the distance, I could hear a baby crying, but it wasn't Angel. It was Owen.

"What?" I asked.

"The baby has been crying all afternoon, Mom," Alex said and held his hands to his ears. "It's driving me nuts."

I exhaled. Owen had been crying incessantly almost since we took him and Amy in. I feared he would wake up Angel, who was taking another nap. I wondered if she was getting ready to stay up all night with all the sleeping she did during the day.

"Mo-o-om, make it stop, please."

I looked down at my son, then kissed the top of his head. "Babies cry, Alex. Sometimes, there isn't much we can do about it. Amy is doing her best."

"I can't stand it, Mom. It never stops."

"Let me go check on them," I said and let go of my son. I walked up the stairs and peeked inside Christine's old room. I found

Amy in there, standing by the window, looking out, while Owen was still in his crib, crying.

I walked to him and picked him up, then approached her by the window.

"Amy?"

She was crying, tears rolling down her cheeks while she stared at the trees outside.

"Amy? Are you okay?"

She sniffled, then shook her head. "I'm...I'm not sure."

Owen quieted down for a few seconds but was still crying.

"I think he might be hungry," I said. I felt his diaper. It needed changing too.

She slumped her shoulders and looked at her feet. "I...I can't... it doesn't really work. I'm not good enough."

I sighed. "It's not easy; believe me, I know. But he needs you."

She shook her head. "He won't eat. When I try, he just keeps on crying and crying."

"It takes time, sweetie, for you two to get to know one another. How about you give it another go, huh?"

She looked at Owen in my arms, her eyes despairing.

"Come on. Sit in the chair, and I'll try and help. I know you can do this, Amy. I'm here for you."

Her eyes teared up again, but she sat down in the armchair I had put in the room for her. I handed her Owen, and she opened her bra. Owen cried a little more but then latched on and started to eat.

"There you go," I said. "He's eating."

Amy moaned. She was obviously uncomfortable. "I think I'm doing it wrong."

"No, you're fine. Just relax, sweetie."

Amy groaned, and Owen let go of the breast again, then cried even louder than before.

"See? It happens every time." She got up and put Owen back in his crib. "I'm not doing it right. I'm not good enough."

Being put back made Owen scream even louder, and Amy held her hands to her ears. "I can't stand it. I can't stand this anymore!"

She screamed, then stormed out of the room. I yelled her name when my phone rang. It was Scott. I had tried to get ahold of him all afternoon, so I had to pick it up. But I couldn't just leave the baby like this.

I grabbed the crying Owen in my arms, then rocked him back and forth while walking out of the room, phone clutched between my shoulder and my ear.

"Scott?"

Chapter 15

O wen was crying helplessly, but I managed to get him to take the pacifier, and soon he calmed down slightly while remaining in my arms. I just prayed that Angel wouldn't wake up as well.

"You called?" Scott asked. He sounded slightly out of breath, and I wondered if he had been running.

"Yes, we need to talk," I said.

"Sure. What's up?"

"I spoke with the detective on Sarah's case today, and they let me take a look at the case file."

Scott went quiet for a second. Owen closed his eyes, and I kept rocking him until he dozed off.

"But that's a good thing, right?" he asked.

"Depends on how you look at it," I said.

"What do you mean?"

"Maybe you tell me, Scott," I said while looking down at the small creature sleeping in my arms. How something so cute and little could cause so much havoc was a mystery to me. "Maybe you should come over so that we can talk properly."

Ten minutes later, he was in my living room. His cheeks were blushing.

"I don't understand," he said, sounding defensive. "You're suddenly looking at me like I'm the criminal here."

"The police seem to think you are. Why do they assume you hurt Sarah?" I asked. "They looked at you immediately, as soon as she went missing, and haven't had their eyes on anyone else. Why is that?"

He went quiet. "I...I..."

"You haven't been completely honest with me, Scott, and you have to if you want my help."

A pause followed before he said: "I know. I'm sorry."

"Okay, good. Tell me what happened. And don't leave anything out this time, please. You were arrested four months ago?"

Scott scoffed. "It was a misunderstanding."

"Even if that's true, it doesn't look good for you."

"It is true. You have to believe me," he said, sounding agitated now. "I didn't hurt her. I would never..."

"Yet Sarah ended up in the hospital with a broken ankle and several bruises on her back. And she told the EMTs that you pushed her down the stairs, Scott."

I could feel the anger rising in me, yet I tried to keep it down.

"It was an accident. She even admitted it later on."

"Yes, the report said she pulled back her testimony the next day while still in the hospital. Then she suddenly said that she had slipped and fallen. But it's a little hard to believe, Scott. Can you see that?"

He groaned. "Of course, I can see that. But it's the truth. We were in a fight, yes. And she did say that she would leave me, and it made me very angry. I did grab her arm, but not hard. She pulled away, and that's when she slipped and fell down the stairs. She was mad at me, and she told the first responders when they arrived that we had been in a fight and that I had grabbed her arm and that she fell down the stairs. She never said I pushed her. They just assumed that's what happened. That's how she explained it to me. Then, once the police came to take her statement after she had been through surgery on her broken ankle, she was able to tell them the truth—that the EMTs had misunderstood her. I am telling you, Eva Rae. I never meant to hurt her. I beat myself up every day over this."

I sighed and rubbed my face. Owen was sound asleep on my arm, and I didn't want to put him back in his crib since I felt he needed closeness, which was why he was so upset all the time. He needed his mother, and right now, I was the closest thing to that. But my arm was getting tired from carrying him, and I would soon have to attend to my own baby's needs. I wished Amy would come back and take him, but I had no idea where she had gone. Hopefully, she had just taken a long walk and would be back later.

"Scott, I have a lot to deal with these days. I'm not sure I can…"

"You don't believe me," Scott sighed resignedly, throwing out his arms. "You're just like everyone else."

"You gotta admit, it sounds odd," I said.

"I wouldn't do something like that. You know me, Eva Rae."

I looked up at him, and our eyes locked. I felt a pinch in my stomach and was overwhelmed with emotions I thought I had forgotten. There was something intense in the way he stared at me that went straight to my heart, and I felt myself ease down. A memory of us kissing flushed my mind and filled me with warmth. I shook it. I couldn't think about those things again. Now was not the time to revisits those old emotions. It was all in the past, and it was best if it stayed there. I couldn't afford to open up the old wounds. I simply had to suppress it.

"Do I?" I asked. "Do I really?"

"I thought so. I mean, we were, after all…."

"I'm gonna stop you right there, Scott. We weren't anything. You made that painfully clear, remember?"

He sighed. "It was a long time ago."

"That we can agree on," I said, fighting to breathe properly—those eyes. I never could resist them or the way he looked at me.

Like he could love me.

A silence followed, and his eyes avoided mine. I placed a hand on his arm.

"Scott? Are you okay?"

"I...I don't know what else to do, where to turn, Eva Rae. I thought you would be different. I thought I could trust you. I guess not."

Now, it was my turn to go quiet. There was something in his voice, a sincerity I couldn't escape. What if he was telling the truth? It would only be a matter of time before the police found him, and then he was toast. No one would believe him.

Did I think he was telling the truth?

I rubbed my tired eyes again, then exhaled deeply. It all seemed so blurry and so confusing. I needed more coffee.

"All right, Scott. I am all for second chances. But no more secrets, okay? You have to disclose everything, or I can't help you. No more surprises."

His face lit up, and he nodded eagerly.

"Of course. Of course."

"Good. Now there was something else in the report that had me thinking—an angle we might be able to use."

Part II

TWO WEEKS LATER

Chapter 16

The heavy door squeaked, and a ray of light hit Sarah Abbey's face. She groaned and squinted, blinded by the sudden brightness. Shuddering, she covered her head and turned her face away, her chains rattling against the pipes while she pushed herself up against the wall behind her.

"Please," she said as the figure moved closer. "Please."

The figure kneeled in front of her. She felt a hand reach for hers. It caressed the top, letting the fingers run over each of her fingers like the person was studying the shape of each and every one of them. The figure then kissed her hand gently while mumbling, "Your skin is so soft."

Sarah shivered and tried to pull it away, but the grip was too tight.

"Please, just let me go."

The other hand reached for her face and caressed her cheek. "You *are* home, my love. You are finally back home."

The remark made Sarah burst into tears. She was so tired, so hungry, and her entire body felt like it was aching in pain. She had been sleeping on the cold floor for days and had lost count of how many had passed. Was it several weeks? It had to be, right?

She had cried, she had screamed, she had slept and hoped she'd wake up, and this nightmare would be over. But as she opened her eyes, again and again, it was all still there. She was still in that awful small room with no windows and no lights: nothing but time to wait for someone to come.

"Why are you keeping me here?" she asked.

The figure tilted its head. "Because I love you. You know that."

It had been the same answer she had received every time she asked, and it made no sense to her. Why, if this person said they loved her, would they treat her like this?

Please, someone must miss me; someone must be looking for me. Please, help me, someone? Anyone?

She had waited and hoped that people would come looking for her, but now she was beginning to lose confidence that they would. She had cut all ties to her family and her past, all her friends when she left her hometown. No one would miss her.

"Don't you love me anymore?" the figure asked, voice cracking.

It was the same every time. She had been asked this very question so many times, and every time, she said she didn't. The figure had slapped her until she finally caved and said that she did. She wasn't going to make that mistake again.

"Of course, I do," she said, sobbing heavily. "I love you so much. You know that. But you can't keep me locked up like this."

The eyes grew weary, and the figure ran a hand through Sarah's hair, holding it, letting it slip slowly through their fingers like every strand had to be admired.

"Do you think I like it? Do you think I want to keep you down here?"

The figure caressed her hair gently while giving her a loving look. Yes, she believed the figure enjoyed keeping her like this, holding her prisoner. She thought they enjoyed that very much. But she wasn't going to say that. She had to keep playing this little game if she wanted to survive. She knew that much.

"It's for your own sake," the figure added. "You know it is. It's what's best for you. You just can't see it. That's why you're lucky to have me."

She nodded, biting back tears and the devastating fear. "Yes, I am very lucky."

That made the figure smile.

"That's my girl."

The figure leaned forward, grabbed her chin, and placed a kiss on her lips. It made her want to gag, but she suppressed it. The figure looked deep into her eyes and gently stroked her face while Sarah struggled not to whimper in fear.

Chapter 17

I drove up the small, quaint street. The stores and restaurants on each side of Park Avenue were packed with people. It was a nice day out, temperatures in the mid-seventies, and sunny. It was a classic February day, with crisp air and clear skies above. To me, that was when Florida was at its best.

"Are you sure she grew up in Winter Park?" Scott asked nervously next to me in the minivan. He looked out at the sidewalk cafés and people strolling in and out of the stores, then turned to face me. His hair had grown a little long in front and fell onto his forehead in a way that framed his eyes cutely. I stared at him, feeling myself get lost for a second, then looked away.

"It just…it doesn't match up with anything she told me," he continued. "She said she was from Athens, Ohio."

I searched for a parking spot along the street, but they all seemed to be occupied. I spotted a couple as they walked up to their car, looking like they were about to leave, and I decided to wait.

"I know, Scott," I said, putting on the blinker to signal that I wanted their parking spot once they left. "I know that's what she told you, but this is what the case file said. This is where she grew up, right outside of Orlando, and this is where her family still lives."

"But why?" he said. "Why would she lie about that? And why haven't I met any of them? If they were here the entire time? Just an hour away?"

I exhaled, hoping these people would hurry up and leave. I didn't have all day. I had left Matt alone with two babies while I did this for Scott, and he wasn't happy about it. It had been two weeks, and still, we hadn't found Amy. She had left that day when Owen cried so helplessly, and no one knew where she was. I was terrified she might have harmed herself, so I involved Matt and Chief Annie in the search. Still, it was like she had vanished from the face of the earth.

Meanwhile, her baby needed her, and I was getting worn out from having to take care of two infants simultaneously. Luckily, Owen had responded well to the bottle and slept better now. Still, it was quite a lot for all of us and putting a strain on our little household. Matt wasn't happy with me, even if he didn't say it much. Frankly, he didn't have to. I could tell by his disapproving looks when I rolled out of bed in the middle of the night to take care of a baby that wasn't ours. But what else was I supposed to do? He thought we ought to call the Department of Children and Families, the DCF, so that they could find a foster home for Owen, but I told him I wasn't ready to give up on Amy yet. I just needed to find her; that's all. I was hoping she would come back on her own, but as the days passed, I felt less confident it was going to happen.

Finally, the car backed out, and the couple left. I slid into the spot and killed the engine, smiling triumphantly. I looked at my watch. We still had ten minutes before meeting with Sarah Abbey's brother. I had contacted everyone in the family, and he was the only one who had gotten back to me after two weeks. He had agreed to meet us for brunch at The Briarpatch. It was supposed to be the best brunch in town, and I was beyond starving. Breastfeeding always made me so hungry, and while my mom and Matt both hoped it would help me shed a couple of pounds—make that fifteen to twenty—my eating habits lately hadn't exactly carried me in that direction, I had to admit.

"Let's find our table," I said and walked up under the yellow awning outside the building that housed the old restaurant. The place was packed, and there was even a line outside, which was a good sign. It told me it was a sought-after place, one worth the long drive. Luckily, I had reserved a table just in case. I walked up to the guy by the entrance and told him my name.

"Thomas, three people."

He nodded and grabbed three menus. "Right over here. Your third party has already arrived."

Chapter 18

THEN:

"Why are you staring at me like that?"

Lynn blinked her eyes. "Sorry? What?"

Jeffrey chuckled. "You've literally been staring at me for like five minutes without saying a word."

Lynn looked down at her notepad, hoping that he wouldn't notice she blushed. "I hardly think it was that long."

"It was. I looked at the clock just now, and it was five minutes."

"Okay, then, I guess I was just…" Lynn trailed off. She couldn't really tell him she had been fantasizing about him, a fantasy she had a lot lately, of him ripping off her clothes and pushing her against the wall. They had been staring into each other's eyes, and it had felt like he was making love with her through them, penetrating her deepest inner self with his gaze. It was intoxicating.

"Where were we?"

"Are you all right, Doc? You seem a little off."

"I'm fine. I just…well, I have a lot on my mind."

"The hubby not giving you enough?"

Her eyes grew wide as she lifted her gaze to meet his again. "Excuse me?"

He grinned. "It's okay. Lots of women your age don't get enough. It's only natural. I can help with that if you like."

His smile was so dashing it felt crushing to her.

"You can't say things like that," she said. "We need to have clear boundaries on this."

"I'm sorry. I was just joking."

She continued, mumbling under her breath, "Besides, I'm not married."

His eyes lit up. "You're not? A woman like you?"

She looked down at her notepad but didn't tell him about the boyfriend, Stan, she had been seeing for the past six years, who didn't believe in marriage and therefore, there would never be one if she stayed with him, which she wasn't sure she would. Especially not at this moment. Heck, they didn't even live together. Not that Lynn wanted him to come live in her new house she had just bought. She liked her peace and quiet and being able to do whatever she wanted to whenever. She didn't answer to anyone.

"So, you were just telling me about your new girlfriend?"

"Yes," he said and leaned back on the couch, placing his hands behind his head, smirking. "And that's when you dozed off and suddenly looked like you could rip my clothes off."

She closed her eyes briefly. "You're overstepping the boundaries again, Jeffrey; we talked about this."

He laughed. "All right; all right. I'll leave you alone. Yes, I told you I had met someone. Her name is Alice. I really like her. Do you want to see a picture of her?"

He pulled out his phone and turned it on, then showed the screen to her before she could tell him that, no, she actually didn't really want to see a picture of the woman who got to go home with him at the end of the day.

"Here."

Lynn stared at the screen, her pulse quickening. She could barely swallow. She stared at the woman with the dyed red hair, alabaster skin, and black-framed glasses on the screen.

She was the spitting image of Lynn herself.

Lynn lifted her gaze and met his while she wondered if he could see the resemblance.

"Cute, right?" he said. "Normally, I like blonde girls, but this one really stood out to me. I met her on this dating site. We've had a few dates, and I think she could be it, Doc. She could be the one. Don't you think?"

Chapter 19

B ryan Abbey was a man in his mid-thirties with long brown curly hair sweeping across his shoulders as he moved and a thick brown beard. He was big and sturdy, and with his many tattoos, he came off as quite intimidating at a first impression. But as soon as he opened his mouth, that changed completely. It became quickly evident to us that he was worried about his sister and missed her greatly. His dark eyes teared up a few times as we spoke about her, and he grew silent for long periods.

"I just don't understand why she would leave us like that," he said as the food had arrived and we dug in. Bryan didn't touch his at first. His eyes remained on me, and his fingers were fiddling with the edge of his black shirt.

"One day, she was there, and the next...gone. That was three years ago now."

"You didn't hear from her at all?" Scott asked.

"She called me a couple of days after she left. She told me she was fine and not to worry. That's why we never went to the police. She sent my parents a letter, explaining that she was fine and not to look for her. It broke their hearts. She left no address and no number to contact her. When our dad got sick, we had no way of letting her know. And now, it's too late. He doesn't remember any of us anymore. We had to place him in a nursing home."

"That's awful," I said.

I shoveled in scrambled eggs like I hadn't eaten in weeks while pondering this new information, wondering what on earth would make a young woman leave her entire family like that without any way for them to contact her.

Scott looked at me and chuckled. I blushed, feeling embarrassed. His warm gaze was still on me after I had swallowed and washed the eggs down with orange juice. I felt his eyes on me a lot when we were together, and it brought back some feelings that I wasn't sure I wanted to let back into my heart. I lifted my gaze, and our eyes met again, making my knees go soft.

I closed my eyes briefly to shake it, then looked away.

"And then...now, a couple of weeks ago, the police contacted my mother and told her Sarah was missing. I can't...and that's how we find out that she was there all along? In Viera? That's so close. We could have..." Bryan trailed off as tears once again filled his eyes. I could tell he was struggling to fight them.

"And you have no idea why she left?" I asked.

He shook his head and drank his Pepsi Max. "I have thought about it for so long. Was it her boyfriend? Was it Tommy? Or was it something between her and our parents? But I can't put the pieces together."

"And that Tommy, he was good to her? Could she have been running from him?" I asked.

"Tommy Waltman was a great guy. He wouldn't lay a hand on my sister. He adored her and worshipped the ground she walked on. Sure, they had their issues. He told me later that they didn't sleep together anymore and that he believed they were drifting apart, but that's hardly a reason for her just to run off like that. It broke his heart. She didn't even leave him a note. I felt so bad for him. He was my best friend."

I looked up. "*Was* your best friend?"

Bryan nodded. "He died six months after she disappeared. He was struck by a car, right over there, actually."

Bryan pointed down Park Avenue.

"On the corner down there by the Panera Bread. He was crossing the street when a car rammed into him, then drove off."

"A hit and run?" I asked.

Bryan nodded. "I know that my sister would have wanted to say goodbye to him at least. But we couldn't find her, so what can you do?"

I looked at Bryan, narrowing my eyes. "And the driver? The hit and run? Was the person ever found?"

Bryan shook his head. "Somewhere out there is a person with a very guilty conscience. I don't even know how you could live with yourself after doing something like that. Even if it was an accident, you still killed someone, you know? You can't just run from something like that."

I couldn't argue with that, and as we said goodbye to Bryan later on, it was all I could think about. How do you hit someone with your car and run from it, then go on living with good conscience? It had to be beyond tough—unless you did it on purpose, of course.

Chapter 20

My house was a regular warzone when I got back home. I opened the door and heard babies crying, not one, but two. Alex was screaming in the living room, yelling at his sister, Christine, while the TV was left on, some cartoon blasting loudly while no one watched. I turned it off, then told Alex and Christine to take their fight upstairs.

Matt came toward me, holding Owen on his arm. His white T-shirt had two big yellow stains on the chest; his hair was tousled and had leftover food stuck to it. I would have laughed had he not looked so profoundly destroyed. I heard Angel crying from the kitchen. Matt saw the frustration on my face as I realized my baby wasn't being cared for.

"I already fed her," he said, "but I had to take care of Owen too. Angel has been crying all morning."

I hurried into the kitchen. It looked like a bomb had gone off. Bowls of cereal everywhere, milk and crumbs smeared on the counter. Meanwhile, Angel was in her Maxi-Cosi rocker chair, strapped down, crying her heart out.

"I was gone three hours, Matt," I said. "I take care of those two babies all day long while you're at work, and you couldn't even do three hours?"

"That's not fair, Eva Rae."

I exhaled while unstrapping my child and grabbing her in my arms. She was helplessly crying while I rocked her from side-to-side until she finally calmed down. Meanwhile, Owen took over, and Matt tried to calm him, but with no luck. With Angel on my hip, I warmed milk for him and handed Matt the bottle. Owen finally calmed down, and soon Matt could put him down for a nap while I cleaned the kitchen with Angel strapped on my chest in her sling. She cried every time I tried to put her down like she was afraid I would leave her and never come back.

Matt sat on a stool and rubbed his temples. "I don't think this is going to work, Eva Rae."

I gave him a look. "What do you mean?"

"We can't have two infants in the house at the same time. It's too much. I can only carry one around at a time. I am not made for this."

"You could have asked Olivia or Christine to help. They would be happy to hold one of them," I said.

"I told Christine to take care of Alex," Matt said. "He spilled milk on his pants during breakfast but refused to change them. That's what they were still arguing about when you came home."

I grabbed a cloth and wiped up some spilled milk mixed with sugary cereal. The sugar had made it almost stiff. I felt so tired and alone. I knew Matt would always step up and try his best to help me out if I asked him to, but I felt alone in the end.

"Can't we call the DCF now?" Matt asked. "They can find a foster home for Owen."

I shook my head. "I can't do that. I am certain Amy is coming back. I won't give up on her."

"Then at least drop whatever it is you're doing with Scott."

I threw the wet cloth in the sink. "I am the only one who has to throw everything down, huh? I was gone three hours, Matt. You're gone all day long, all week long, even sometimes the weekends as well."

Matt rubbed his eyes and shook his head. "Can't you see we're in over our heads here? Why is it so important to help this guy out anyway? It's not like you were friends or anything. Is it really worth it? I mean, look at the house."

"I am helping Scott because I can," I said. "Because he needs it. The house is fine. No one died because of a little mess."

He shook his head. "There's more to it than that. Don't you think I've seen the way he looks at you?"

I flinched. I didn't think anyone else had noticed. I looked at the floor and turned away from him, facing the sink.

"I don't know what you're talking about."

Matt scoffed, then left the kitchen, mumbling, "Sure, you do."

Chapter 21

Lily grabbed her water bottle and drank from it, still while running on the treadmill. Cocoa Beach Health and Fitness, where she worked out on Saturdays, Tuesdays, and Thursdays, was packed as usual.

Lily wiped her forehead with a towel, then stopped running and moved on to the bike, where she worked another fifteen minutes until she moved on to lifting weights. She looked at herself in the mirrors when she spotted someone behind her and dropped the weight.

It was him again—the guy from the café.

Their eyes met in the mirror, and she could tell that he blushed. Why was he looking at her that way? It made her feel uncomfortable. Lily gave him a strange look, one to make him back off, then returned to her weightlifting.

Maybe she was just being paranoid. After all, the guy was allowed to work out in the same place as her. Everyone from Cocoa Beach worked out here when they didn't run on the beach or surf.

She just didn't care much for the way he stared at her. There was something creepy about that look in his eyes. Maybe it was just the fact that he constantly stared at her that made her freak out.

He might just think you're hot.

Lily continued her lifting while keeping an eye on him in the mirror. She saw him stop working out, then grab his stuff and leave. Relieved at this, she finished her session, but as she left and walked outside to the parking lot, she saw him sitting in his car. The motor was running, but he wasn't moving. He was just sitting there, still staring at her. It made her shiver, and she rushed to her own car and got in. She took off, speeding and hurrying through an intersection just as the light turned red. Still speeding and with her heart racing, she looked in the rearview mirror and noticed his car had stopped at the light.

He wouldn't be able to follow her anymore.

She took a deep breath, thinking she had escaped him. Yet she couldn't shake the uneasy feeling, and as soon as she got home, she called her boyfriend, Peter.

"Can you come over? I don't want to be alone tonight."

They hadn't been doing so well lately, and if she was honest, she had been avoiding his calls. But now, she needed him.

"Be right there."

She stood by the window, looking out through the thin see-through curtains, jumping at every car that drove by. Peter arrived fifteen minutes later, and she threw herself into his arms. He lifted her and carried her to the couch. As he helped her get her shirt off, she glanced briefly at the window and then screamed.

"What?" Peter said, jumping up.

She held her shirt up in front of her breasts, then pointed. "There was someone out there. He was looking in at us. He was watching us."

Peter rushed to the window and pulled the thin curtain aside.

"I don't see anyone."

"But he was there," she said, her voice shaking. "I swear, Peter. I am not making this up. There was someone out there, watching us having sex."

Chapter 22

I swung my minivan around in the cul-de-sac and parked in the driveway. I sat for a few seconds, staring at the mansion in front of me, taking a few deep breaths to prepare. I had gotten myself quite worked up on my way there, thinking of all the things I wanted—no needed—to say. I had been up most of the night, thinking about it, and made the decision this morning.

I walked to the back, got Owen out in his car seat, and carried him up toward the front door with the frosted glass and beautifully carved-in palm trees. I stared at the doorbell for a few seconds, gathering my courage, then pressed it. Shortly after, the door swung open, and Kim's face appeared.

I lifted Owen, who was still sleeping in his car seat.

"Kim. Meet your grandson, Owen. Owen, this is your grandmother."

Kim stared at me with huge eyes. She didn't even look down at the baby, and then she tried to close the door on me. I placed my hand on it and pushed it back open, then stepped inside the big hall.

"Eva Rae Thomas," she said. "You can't just…you can't just…"

Finally, her eyes landed on the child, and something seemed to happen. She couldn't lift her eyes to look at me and just stood there, nostrils flaring.

"He's your grandson, for crying out loud," I said. "Amy has run away, and we can't find her. I can't take care of him forever. I have an infant of my own, remember?"

Kim looked at Owen, and it was obvious she was struggling. She closed her eyes and shook her head.

"No. We can't."

"Why on earth not? Give me one good reason. You have a big house. You don't even work."

Kim shook her head. "I'm sorry, but…"

"Okay, so you're angry with Amy, but why take it out on the baby? He needs you. He needs a family right now. If Amy never comes back, then…"

"No," Kim said, holding a hand to her chest. She was biting back her tears. "I am sorry. We can't. Phil is going to…" she paused, breathed, then said, "I need you to leave now."

"Come on, Kim, how can you be so…?"

She pointed a finger at me, her lips quivering as she spoke. "You don't know anything about me. Now leave, please."

I exhaled. I had really hoped to convince her to take care of her grandson and appeal to her better side. Now, it just seemed like she didn't have one.

"Okay, can you at least tell me who the father is? Maybe he can take care of Owen."

Her eyes grew dark. "We don't know who he is. Amy wouldn't tell us. Now, please, leave."

I looked into her eyes, scrutinizing them, trying to find some sense to what she was saying and doing. I couldn't for the life of me understand her motives. The kid was the cutest thing in the world, and he was all she had left of her daughter right now. Why wouldn't she want him?

"Kim, come on, can't we at least…?"

She shook her head. "Please, leave before I call the police."

I looked down at Owen, feeling sorry for him. By the time the door closed behind me, and I walked down the driveway, he was wailing loudly.

I couldn't blame him. I was beginning to wonder when it was my turn to scream.

Chapter 23

$\mathbf{T}$HEN:

"Guess what I did over the weekend?"

Jeff's eyes gleamed as he looked at Lynn. She felt her heart drop. He was so happy at this moment, but it wouldn't last long. She had something to say to him that wouldn't be pleasant for either of them. But it had to be done.

"Jeff," she said.

His smile grew stiff as he realized how serious she was.

"Yes? What's up, Doc? What's with the face?"

Lynn sighed. Her feelings for him were so hard to deny. She had talked to her supervisor about it, and he had told her to monitor it closely and refer Jeff to another therapist if she wasn't able to keep them at bay. It was all about the patient and making sure he got the help he needed. She was now wondering if she had let it go too far already.

She looked down at her notepad. "So...my mom called yesterday."

He wrinkled his forehead. "Y-your mom?"

"Yes, my mother. And she had an interesting story to tell me."

"Yeah?"

"She told me she had met one of my friends. That he came to her house and that he said we worked together."

"A-and?" Jeff asked, his voice trembling.

"And her description of this person sounded a lot like you."

Jeff's eyes grew wide, and then he looked at the floor. A long silence followed.

"Jeff? Can you look at me, please?"

He didn't. His eyes remained glued to the floor.

She sighed. "Jeff, you can't do that. You can't visit my mother."

"I...I am sorry. I just...well...I just like you so much, and I..." He stopped, then shook his head. "No, I am not gonna say that."

Lynn narrowed her eyes. "Now, you kind of have to, don't you?"

He lifted his gaze, and his eyes met hers again. The look in them made her soften up and lean back with a compassionate sigh.

"I'm kind of obsessing over you," he said, fiddling with his fingers. "I've been driving past your house and stalking you on Facebook. I don't know why I do these things; it's just...I think about you a lot."

Lynn smiled. "It's okay, Jeff. It's normal. It's called transference. It will pass. It has nothing to do with love, what you're feeling for me. It's some unresolved emotions from your past and possibly childhood that we might need to dig into. There could be some unresolved issues you might benefit from looking at more closely. That's all it is. Just try and dial down on the craziness, okay? No going past my house; no going to any of my family members. No looking at my Facebook profile. It can't happen again, or I'll have to refer you to another therapist."

He nodded while tears were springing to his eyes. He wiped them away with a swift movement.

"Do you feel it too?"

Lynn swallowed. She looked down at her notepad, taking a few deep breaths. "What I feel is irrelevant. This is about you."

That made his face light up, and his lips curl into a smirk. "So, you do, huh?"

"I didn't say that," she said.

"You know your lower lip slightly vibrates when you're lying, right? Just like it is right now."

She lifted her eyes and looked into his. "Jeff. It can never happen. Do you understand that?"

His shoulders slumped, and he leaned back.

"Okay. I hear you. Forgive me, Doc."

Chapter 24

I'm gonna die in here, aren't I? This is it for me. I'm gonna rot away in this
hellhole and never see sunlight again.

Sarah Abbey lifted her head in the darkness. The chains rattled
behind her as she pulled them in an attempt to stretch her arms.
She missed seeing sunlight; she missed feeling the fresh air on her
face. She wondered how long she had been trapped in this place
and realized she didn't even know if it was day or night. She had
completely lost track of time. All she could do was wait for her
kidnapper to show up. It seemed like an eternity went by between
the visits. Not that Sarah looked forward to them, since she was
terrified of what her kidnapper wanted—if this person wanted to
hurt her or maybe even kill her, but it was the only break in the
everlasting darkness.

Sarah let her hands run across the floors, feeling her way
around, trying to find the toilet bucket in the back corner. Her
hands swept across the dirty tile floors, touching sand and dust and
trying to avoid the dead roach she had accidentally touched the day
before when looking for the bucket. She had tried to memorize
where it was so that it wouldn't happen again. As her fingers

searched through the wilderness, the chains were clanking loudly behind her, and she suddenly felt something between her fingers, something that definitely wasn't dirt or dust—or a roach. She grabbed it between her fingers and held it up, feeling it from the flat bottom to the pointy top.

A nail. Definitely a nail.

Sarah burst into laughter as she felt it again and again, just to make sure she wasn't imagining things. Panting in excitement and forgetting all about her quest to make it to the toilet bucket, she returned to her spot. She tried to poke the pointy end of the nail into the chains, fiddling with it, feeling them, and hoping she could find some kind of opening, a keyhole maybe where the chains were locked together or something, anything. There had to be some way of opening them.

Right?

Desperately, she poked the nail into the chain, but she couldn't find an opening. Sarah could hear her own loud breathing in her head and her pulse as it pounded in her ears. The hope she had made her suddenly frantic and caused her to sob uncontrollably when she didn't succeed in her quest. She pulled the chains in anger and growled loudly in despair, then slumped to the floor, nail still clutched in her hand.

Then she cried. Salty tears rolled down her face as she felt how weak she was from the lack of enough food to feed her poor body and from being kept in the same position so long while not moving much. Her brain felt foggy, and it was hard to think clearly.

I'll never get out of this place!

Sarah took a deep breath, trying to calm herself. Panicking didn't help anything. It only made her more confused and desperate, and then she couldn't think straight.

Sarah sat back, head leaned against the wall, as she had done so many times before, but this time with the nail tightly clutched between her hands. She felt the tip of it with her thumb, poking the skin.

That's when she heard footsteps on the other side of the door.

Approaching footsteps that soon stopped outside it, and then there was the well-known fumbling behind it before it opened slowly, and the light once again blinded Sarah. As she regained her sight, she looked into the face of her kidnapper, who was smiling broadly and wearing the look of a madman.

Chapter 25

I fed Owen his bottle and put him down for his nap, then took a deep breath, realizing that I had succeeded in putting down both babies, and the house was completely quiet since all the rest of the children were in school.

A small piece of unexpected heaven.

I left the babies in their cribs, walking away as quietly as possible, then hurried down the stairs, poured myself a cup of coffee, and just took in the silence, enjoying it for as long as it would last. I couldn't stop thinking about Amy and her parents. What had gone so wrong between them? Could it just be the embarrassment of her becoming pregnant at only fifteen? Was that enough to entirely cut your ties to your own daughter and grandson? Could anyone really be that cruel?

I shook my head and sipped my cup, praying under my breath for Amy and that she was somewhere safe. I had driven by the abandoned house she had been hiding in earlier, but she wasn't there. Christine didn't know where she was either, she said. In the beginning, I thought she knew but just wouldn't tell me, so I had been angry with her for keeping it from me, but I knew now that she was telling the truth. It was like Amy had vanished. Matt and his colleagues had put out a search for her, but still with no luck. I had also written in the local Facebook group for people living in Cocoa Beach and told them to look out for her, but still no news.

How far could a fifteen-year-old girl go with no money or even a phone?

A thought entered my mind, and I spoke it out into the silence of the kitchen.

"The father. She could be hiding with him. If only I could find out who he is."

I sat by my laptop, then went on Instagram to see if I could find her profile. I found her through Christine's followers and scrolled through her posts. She hadn't posted anything new in a long time. The last post was a picture of her in a bathing suit on the beach that was obviously taken before she became pregnant. I read through the comments, then saw one from a boy. He wrote that she was gorgeous. I clicked his profile and looked at his pictures. Lots of them had Amy in them, and in one, they were kissing.

Bingo!

He had to be her boyfriend. I could tell he was a kid from the high school since he was wearing a hoodie with the Cocoa Beach High logo on it and had posted pictures of him playing for the lacrosse team. He couldn't be hard to find. It took me all of three seconds to find out he lived on a side street from Minutemen Causeway, our main road. He wasn't in Christine's grade level since I knew most of the kids there. He looked older, too, so probably a year or two above was my guess.

He had to be Owen's dad, I thought to myself. Was that where Amy was hiding? It was certainly possible.

I stared at his face on my screen when an email popped up and took my mind elsewhere. It was from my dad. He was an extremely skilled hacker, and I asked him to help me find the surveillance footage from Park Avenue in Winter Park three years ago when Sarah's boyfriend, Tommy, was struck by a car.

He wrote:

HERE YOU GO. PIECE OF CAKE.

Piece of cake, yeah, right! I thought to myself. It was three years old;

it couldn't have been easy to obtain. Most traffic cameras deleted footage after as little as twenty-four hours, so it had to have been from a store or maybe even from the police file. Not that I wanted to know. We had an agreement that he didn't tell me how he got the things for me since it could get me in trouble if his ways weren't done entirely by the law. I didn't have to know about it.

He ended the email:

SEE YOU THIS WEEKEND.

I sighed. I had completely forgotten that I had said yes to my dad, grandmother, and half-brother to come down and see the baby this coming weekend. With the house a complete and utter mess and our living situation chaotic, to put it mildly, I wasn't sure I could manage that. I hadn't even had my own mother come over. I had been going to her place, so she wouldn't see and criticize our living situation. If they all came down from Amelia Island, were they expecting to stay with us?

Probably.

"If they don't mind sleeping on the couch and mattresses on the floor of the living room, I guess we could make it work, but Matt is going to kill me," I mumbled to myself, then opened the file my dad had sent me and poured myself another cup of coffee to keep me going.

Chapter 26

"Scott. Come in. Hurry."

Scott looked at me with his usual smirk, the same one that always made me weak in the knees.

"Someone's excited to see me," he said.

"Don't flatter yourself."

I closed the door behind him, then pulled him to my laptop and poured him a cup of coffee that I handed to him. I waited for a second to make sure the babies were still sound asleep, and when I heard nothing, I looked at him.

"I came as soon as you called," he said. "What's going on?"

His green eyes sparkled in the light coming from the window. He had very, *very* nice eyes, and lips, and…

Stop it, Eva Rae!

I removed my gaze from his gorgeous face, then looked at the screen instead. His elbow touched mine as he moved closer to be able to look over my shoulder. It was odd to feel him this close to me again. He smelled just like he had back then. I tried hard not to, but I couldn't help blushing.

Would you give it up already? You're getting married, remember?

Shaking away my own weakness, I focused on the screen in front of me and the video I had just watched.

"This is surveillance footage from the day that Tommy was killed by a hit and run," I said.

Scott looked like he wasn't sure he followed me.

"The guy who dated Sarah when she lived in Winter Park?" I elaborated, trying to get him up to speed. "The guy the brother told us about?"

"Ah, yes, of course."

"Now, I'm going to play it for you. It's tough stuff, so brace yourself. You're about to see a man die. Can you handle it?"

He smiled. "Of course, I can."

"Okay, here we go."

I pressed the space bar, and the video started to roll. On the screen, we saw the main street, Park Avenue, and I pointed.

"There. This is Tommy. Now, look at him as he continues to walk down the street."

Scott nodded and leaned forward, brushing up against me. It felt like it was almost on purpose. What was he playing at?

"Anyway, look at him walking down this part of the sidewalk, and then there...he decides to cross the road, then look at the car here."

We both watched as Tommy glanced briefly over his shoulder, then decided to cross the street. In the same second, a car came toward him and hit him head-on.

Scott made a squeal that made me stop the video. I looked at him and saw that his eyes were terrified. I recognized that look. Seeing someone get killed, knowing it was real, could be a lot to handle.

"Are you okay?"

He placed his hands on his head, then nodded after a few seconds of silence. "Yeah, yeah. I mean, I knew it was going to happen...but..."

"It can still be a lot," I said. "We don't have to watch more."

He grimaced. "It's okay. I'll be fine. I just..."

"Let's take a closer look first at what went on before he was hit,"

I said, then scrolled back in the file and started it again. "See, when I first watched it, I only focused on the hit itself and when the car leaves the scene like the police probably did. But you can only see the front of the car in the corner of the video, and it's not visible as it drives away—at least not enough to identify it. But then, I went back a few minutes on the timeline and saw something interesting."

"What?"

I played it. "Here, we see Tommy a few minutes before he's hit, still walking down the sidewalk. And look at what is right behind him." I pointed at the screen where the front of a car was poking out in the corner. "Doesn't that look like the same car?"

He stared at it, and I started the video again. "Now, Tommy goes into this store here, and a few seconds later, he comes back out, but see what happens in the meantime. The car drives past the store; tell me that isn't the same car," I said, and Scott nodded.

"It sure looks like it."

"When Tommy comes back out, look who just happens to drive up across the street from him and stop."

Scott stared, eyes wide. "Waiting for him."

"Yes, and now that he continues, it follows him, parking behind him every time he stops to look at store windows. And then, when he crosses the street?"

"It accelerates," Scott said, "and hits him."

"Exactly. Now, the police probably only focused their investigation on the seconds he was hit and the minutes after, trying to recognize the car or the driver when it was barely in the shot. But they didn't think to look at what happened ahead of the hit."

"I'll be..." Scott said. "So, you're saying it wasn't a coincidence?"

"Nope. It was on purpose. Tommy was intentionally murdered by whoever drove this car."

"Huh."

"The question is, of course, still, who was behind that wheel? And I think I might have an answer to that as well—or at least a clue we can pursue."

Scott smiled. "I hoped you'd say something like that. That's why

I came to you. And I take it you believe that whoever killed Tommy has also taken Sarah? Is that it?"

I nodded and sipped my coffee, secretly enjoying having impressed him. "It's my theory that if we find him, we find Sarah, yes."

"So, what is it?" he asked, clasping his hands excitedly. "The clue?"

I smiled secretively, then pointed at the screen where I had stopped the footage at the best picture of the car's right side. The image was grainy and of terrible quality, but I could still see enough.

"It's a truck," I said and pointed. "And not just any ordinary truck. Look at the stripe on the side. What's written there?"

Scott looked closer. "Skyranger?"

"Exactly. It's a Ford Skyranger. I've looked it up, and Ford only made twenty trucks of this type back in the nineties. And there's only one registered with the DMV in the Orlando area. It's far-fetched, but at least we have one."

Scott smiled his handsome smile once again, and I felt myself getting pulled in by it. He saw me staring, and his eyes grew serious. Then he leaned forward and closed his eyes.

I gasped.

"Scott!"

I pulled back and pushed him. He opened his eyes and looked at me as I jumped down from my stool.

"What do you think you're doing?"

"I'm sorry," he said, his eyes deep with regret. "I am so sorry. I just...well...I guess I just got pulled back to the old days for a second. Don't...don't put anything into it. Please."

I scrutinized his face to make sure he wasn't lying to me, then eased up.

"I am about to be married, Scott. Don't you ever try anything like that again. Do you hear me? Never."

Chapter 27

She ordered the fresh-caught tuna and Peter a burger. They were sitting close together on the outside deck at Coconuts on the Beach. Lily had been with him almost constantly since the incident where she was certain the guy from the café was outside her house, looking in. The more she thought about it, though, the more she had come to terms with the fact that she had probably just imagined it because of what had happened earlier at the fitness club. She had thought she saw him there. That had to be why.

"Can I get you another one of those?" the woman in the tight tank top asked and pointed at Peter's empty beer glass. He nodded, and she refilled it with a sweet smile. Lily felt a sudden discomfort and leaned into a kiss. Feeling Peter close made Lily feel more at ease, and as their lips parted, Peter caressed her cheek gently, looking into her eyes.

"I've missed this. Us."

"I'm sorry. I've been busy," she said, looking down at her drink. "You know with the record deal and all that. I have to finish writing the last songs."

"I know. You're becoming a big star. And I get to say that I'm with you. I knew you before you became a household name. How cool is that?"

Peter took another bite of his burger, and Lily sat up straight. She had lost her appetite. She had given their relationship a lot of thought lately and wasn't sure she wanted to be with him, or anyone for that matter, once she started her new career. She couldn't have anyone holding her back from her big breakthrough, and this could be it. But how do you tell someone that? She hated to have to hurt him. She cared for him. On the other hand, she had worked to get this record deal for most of her life, and she couldn't have any distractions. This was it. This was her shot.

She smiled awkwardly at him, then drank from her soda while looking away, avoiding Peter's eyes. As she shot a look across the wooden porch area, her eyes suddenly locked with those from someone sitting at the tiki bar.

Lily could barely breathe.

"What the…"

Lily reached for Peter and grabbed his arm.

"What's wrong? Lily? You look like you're about to be sick."

Lily swallowed, trying to push down the knot in her stomach, then leaned closer to him. "Look over there at the guy sitting at the bar."

The guy had stopped looking at her and was paying for his beer, handing the bartender a bill. He then stood to his feet and was about to leave.

Lily got up. "Hey, mister!"

"What are you doing?" Peter asked. "Lily?"

But she was gone and already standing right in front of the guy as he turned to walk away. Startled, he looked down at her.

"Are you following me? Huh?" she asked, heart pounding. "I keep seeing you everywhere. At the café, at the fitness club, outside my house? Are you some kind of creepy stalker, huh?"

Peter came up behind her. This guy was double his age, but probably only half as fast. Plus, Peter was big. Seeing this, the guy lifted his hands in the air.

"Listen, lady. I don't know what you're talking about. I've just been sitting here enjoying my beer."

She was in his face. "I don't believe you. I see you everywhere. I think I saw you outside of my house one morning when going to work too. I don't like you."

The guy stared at her, his eyes piercing into hers like he couldn't take them away from her. They stood like that for a few seconds longer than felt comfortable before the guy finally looked away.

"I was just leaving," he said.

Lily felt so angry she could scream. Sensing this, Peter placed a hand on her shoulder. "Let's just go. He's a nobody."

She scoffed while the guy left.

"Yeah. You're right. He's no one."

Chapter 28

A cold hand reached out and touched Sarah's cheek, caressing it gently. A set of compassionate eyes looked into hers.

"You are so beautiful."

"I feel awful."

"Are you not feeling any better? Yesterday, you were coughing, and I was worried."

Sarah stared at her jailer, blinking. The hand still touched her skin gently, rubbing up and down against it as you'd do to a child or a loved one. The feeling made Sarah tremble.

Her jailer narrowed their eyes. "You're fine, aren't you?"

Sarah lowered her head. She felt the nail inside of her fist, the pointy end poking her thumb.

"I think you are."

"Why do you care?" Sarah asked, looking up again.

Her jailer looked surprised at the question.

"I care for you."

"You have a strange way of showing that. If you cared for me, you'd let me go home."

Her jailer tilted their head and placed both hands on Sarah's shoulders. "But you are home. This is where you belong. With me."

The raving insanity in the words leaving the jailer's mouth caused Sarah to despair. It made no sense why she was being kept here. Sarah felt tears sting her eyes. A couple escaped and rolled down her cheeks.

"Please," she said. "Just let me go."

"Ah-ah, no can do," the jailer said, wagging a finger in front of Sarah's face. The jailer leaned forward and placed a set of wet lips first on Sarah's forehead, then on her mouth. Sarah shivered again.

"It's okay," the jailer said, caressing her cheek, leaning their forehead against hers. "Everything is going to be okay."

Sarah couldn't stop crying. She was so tired, exhausted, and had no idea how to deal with this strange person. All she knew was that she needed to get out of there.

Now.

Sarah lifted her hand with the nail in it, slid it to her fingertips, then jammed it into her jailer's chest. The sound it made as it pierced through the flesh was nauseating, but much to Sarah's surprise, she seemed to be so fueled by anger, she barely noticed. Her jailer let out a roar, and blood spurted out from the wound. Her jailer fell to the tiles, gasping and panting. Sarah acted quickly. She crawled on top of the person and slammed her fists into her jailer's head until her jailer stopped moving. Then she stuck her hands into all the pockets and pulled out a set of keys. She then unlocked her chains with the keys, fumbling nervously with them as her jailer moaned in pain. Sarah almost dropped the keys before she finally succeeded in getting loose and could move her hands freely. She didn't think twice but ran out of the small room, not looking back at her jailer on the floor. She ran down a hallway and spotted a set of stairs at the end of it. She almost gasped as she saw the sunlight coming down from above—almost like heaven was calling out for her, showing her the way.

Freedom, at last. At last.

Chapter 29

T HEN:
    "Oh-oh, I do not like the look on that face. What's up?"

Lynn sat up straight in her chair as Jeff stormed in and sat down across from her. His eyes were red, and he hadn't shaved in what looked like days. As usual, he was wearing a suit, but something about the way he wore it told her he hadn't cared much for dressing himself this morning before going to work. He usually came to her in the late afternoons, after he finished at the office.

He looked like a mess.

Jeff exhaled, then sniffled.

"Take your time," she said, trying to create a calm atmosphere, one where he felt safe. She couldn't let him know how much it upset her, seeing him like this, how it made her stomach turn into a knot and her heart race. "There's no rush."

Jeff nodded, then scratched his neck and took a couple of deep breaths, very obviously calming himself. Then he leaned forward and threw out his arms.

"She left me."

Lynn exhaled. "The new girl you were dating? Alice?"

He scoffed. "Can you believe it?"

No, she couldn't, but she couldn't say that. To her, Jeff was such a wonderful and perfect guy. She couldn't understand why anyone would ever leave him or even want to hurt him. He was so handsome and charming, and to her, he had it all. But she couldn't say that.

"Tell me what happened," she said instead.

He shook his head. "I don't know why I even bother. These women they're…they're…" he slapped his hand onto his thigh, startling Lynn. He then clenched his fist and said, "I hate her."

"Tell me what happened. When did she break up with you?" she repeated.

"I came home from work two days ago, and she had her bags packed. We've only been dating for five months, but she had basically moved into my apartment and slept there every night. I thought she was the one; I really thought she was."

"Did she say anything? Did she give you an explanation?" Lynn asked, not allowing herself to get as riled up on the outside as she felt on the inside. Who did this girl think she was?

"She'd been with someone else, she told me. Someone from her workplace and she was going to be with him instead. Just like that."

"She cheated on you?" Lynn spat, sounding angrier than she intended.

"Yes, can you believe it?" Jeff said. "She cheated on me."

Lynn shook her head and wrote on her notepad. It was odd that a guy like Jeff couldn't find himself a nice girl to settle down with. Why were these women so stupid?

His wet eyes locked with hers as she lifted her gaze. "How am I supposed to live without her? Do you think I'll ever find a girlfriend again? Someone who'll want to stay with me?"

That broke her heart. This was the second breakup she had gone through with him. She nodded, leaned over, and placed a hand on his knee.

"Of course, you will."

The hand lingered on his knee while he stared into her eyes. She felt a pinch in her stomach, and her entire body warmed up. Then she removed the hand, pulling it back quickly, blushing.

"I'm ugly," he said. "No one will have me."

That made Lynn chuckle. He gave her a puzzled look.

"You find it amusing?"

"No, it's just that…well, you're really handsome," Lynn said. "I hope you realize that. You're to die for."

That made him smile, almost smirking. "Really? You think so?"

"Sure."

"You'd actually die for me?"

She paused and felt a furrow grow between her eyes. "Well… figuratively speaking, of course. It's a saying."

He leaned back on the couch. "Huh."

"Why do you say that?"

"Not for anything. I just…well…you want to sleep with me, don't you? I can see it in your eyes, the way you look at me."

Lynn took another deep breath. "We've been through this, Jeff. You can't say stuff like that."

"But you do, don't you?"

"It's of no importance whether or not I want to sleep with you, Jeff. You're my client. It will never happen."

He smiled and nodded. "But you want to. It's okay, Doc. I won't tell anyone. Your secret is safe with me."

Chapter 30

The air between us was thick and the atmosphere awkward in the minivan as we drove toward Orlando and, more precisely, Winter Park. I kept thinking about the way Scott had leaned in toward me and tried to kiss me the day before, and every time I looked at him, I felt awful. I couldn't believe him. I thought he loved Sarah. The air between us was so strange, so tense, I felt like screaming. We both reached for our coffee at the same time, and our hands brushed up against each other.

"I'm sorry," I said and pulled mine away.

"No. No, you go," he said.

"It's okay."

Then silence followed. Neither of us grabbed our coffees. I cleared my throat and passed a truck. We had barely spoken all morning. He came to my house so we could drive there in my car, and I could hardly look him in the eyes. I was frustrated with him yet had to admit, I was also secretly flattered. But it was wrong on so many levels, and now I feared it had ruined everything between us.

"I feel bad," he suddenly said as we left Cocoa Beach and took the beachline. I accelerated the car, then sipped my latte that we had bought at a drive-thru Starbucks on the way.

"You do?" I asked, startled at this sudden honesty from him.

He nodded. I spotted a dead raccoon on the side of the road and felt sick at the sight of the blood.

"I shouldn't have tried to kiss you." He hid his face in his hands. "I can't believe myself. Here I am, worried sick about Sarah, and then I go and pull something like that."

I felt relieved. With him saying this, we could hopefully put it behind us. I was going to try to, at least.

"Your secret is safe with me," I said, wanting to change the subject. It felt uncomfortable talking about this. "Don't worry. You had a weak moment. We all have them from time to time. The important thing is to find Sarah. That's all we need to focus on right now. She knew someone from her past might catch up to her one day, or she wouldn't have said what she did to you. That's our focus. If this same guy killed her boyfriend back then, then we might find him through that truck."

He turned and looked at me. "You're amazing; have I told you that?"

That made me smile. "Really? No. But you don't have to, Scott. I'm not doing this for you, but for her." It wasn't a total lie. But it was a lie. I was doing it for him, mostly. But he didn't need to know that.

"No, I'm serious. You're the only one who has believed me. Everyone else thought I hurt her, even my own family. I don't know what I would have done if you had refused to help me."

That made me blush. I wasn't sure what to say.

"I mean, you have enough on your plate as it is with two infants and all those other kids. I don't know how you do it."

I thought about Owen and Angel back at the house. I had persuaded my mom to take them both today, even though it meant having her inside my messy house and facing weeks of criticism for it afterward. I felt bad for asking her to do this. It was a long time since she last had an infant, and she wasn't exactly used to the chaos that came with it. At first, she had looked at me like I was nuts for even asking, but somehow—Lord only knows how—I had managed to talk her into it. I might have accidentally promised to go to a vegan health conference of some sort with her in a few weeks in Orlando. I was probably going to regret saying yes to it, but how horrible could it be?

It's going to be awful, and you know it. Your mom is going to try to persuade you to live healthier and exercise more, and she'll always be on your case while you're there, telling you if only you ate this or did this, then you'd live a healthier life.

"All it takes are a few small adjustments."

That's what she always told me.

"Just cut out the sugar in your coffee, and drink water instead of soda. Eat a piece of fruit instead of the cookies you always stuff yourself with."

Oh, yes, it was going to get horrible, and I'd have to eat quinoa and kale all day, but so be it. If this could help us find Sarah Abbey, then I was willing to make the sacrifice. Besides, one of the children could happen to come down with something right on the day I was supposed to go, right? It was possible. Then, naturally, I couldn't go. My mom would have to understand that. Of course, she would.

"So, this guy has that type of truck?" Scott asked as we came closer to Orlando and could see the signs leading to the airport.

"He bought it in 2010, yes. For twenty-five thousand. The truck is from 1991."

"And does he still have it? Could he be our guy?"

"That's what we're about to find out," I said. "I haven't exactly told him we're coming. I just found his name and address in the DMV records. His name is Jeffrey Johnson."

Chapter 31

"Is this it? Are you sure?"

Scott peeked out the window of the minivan. I had parked by the house and killed the engine. I squinted my eyes to better see against the bright sun that stood right above us.

"What in the..."

Scott got out, and I followed him, slamming the car door shut behind me. There was barely anything left of the house in front of us. It had very obviously been ravaged in a devastating fire. The roof was completely gone, and there was nothing left but the char-coaled walls. I got the feeling it had been a nice house before it burned down. All the neighboring houses were very exclusive—cute, older Florida houses from the nineteen twenties, several of them two-stories, with lots of space and big yards. The entire neighborhood surrounded Lake Sylvan, where you could go fishing or boating.

"You sure you got it right?" Scott asked.

I looked at my phone at the address, then at the mailbox where the house number was still written. "Yes, that's it."

"I'll be..." Scott said. He glared toward the garage or the little that was left of it. "You think the car was in there when it burned down?"

"Excuse me? Can I help you?"

A woman in high heels came from the house across the street and approached us, tapping along on the asphalt. She was gorgeous with her long hair in a ponytail, light makeup, and expensive blue business suit. I felt inadequate and unaccomplished in my old baggy jeans.

I smiled. "Yes, maybe you can. I'm Eva Rae Thomas, and this is Scott Benton."

I reached out my hand, and we shook.

"Isabella Hayton."

"We're looking for a Jeffrey Johnson."

Her smile faded, and her lips stiffened.

"Jeff?"

"Yes, he lives here according to DMV records, but…"

She swallowed. "Jeff…did use to live here. But I'm afraid…he died in the fire."

I froze. "Oh, no. That's awful. I am so sorry. Did you know him well?"

She nodded. "I'm actually his sister. We bought these houses in the same neighborhood to be close together."

"How awful. I am so sorry. What happened?"

She shook her head with a deep exhale. "They don't know. It was probably caused by something electrical; at least, that was the conclusion in the report. It happened at night. Jeff was sleeping. He had taken a couple of sleeping pills as he sometimes did, so he didn't wake up."

She sniffled and fought her tears, then placed a hand under her nose for a few seconds like it calmed her down.

"How long ago was this?"

"It happened four years ago," she said. "Can you believe it? We're still fighting the insurance company to get the money. They keep dragging it out."

Four years ago? Tommy was killed two and a half years ago. It couldn't have been Jeffrey Johnson who drove the truck then.

"That's tough," I said and placed a hand on the woman's shoulder. Isabella looked at me and nodded.

"Why are you looking for him?"

"We're actually looking for his car," I said. "A Ford Skyranger. One of the rarest pick-up trucks Ford ever made."

I showed her a picture of the truck from the Internet. Isabella's face lit up. "Yeah, that's Jeff's truck. He loved it so much—ugliest thing in the world if you ask me, but he never did care for my opinion."

"So, he did own one?"

She nodded. "Yes. But it was in his garage when it burned down, so it was lost in the fire."

"Do you know if Jeff was ever in an accident with that car?" I asked, even though I knew it didn't fit with the timeline.

Isabella paused. She gave me a strange look. "Who are you people? Why are you asking all these questions?"

I showed her my FBI badge. "We're just investigating an old case. Two and a half years ago, a man was hit by a truck in downtown Winter Park. It was a Ford Skyranger like Jeff's."

She shook her head. "So, you thought my brother killed him?"

"We're investigating what happened; that's all. The car led us here in our search. But if Jeffrey died in the fire four years ago, then it couldn't have been him."

She scoffed. "I can't believe you people, coming here and asking these questions after he is dead. Have you no shame?"

"I…just said that…"

Isabella didn't stay to hear me out. She turned around and walked away, her high heels clicking loudly. Scott came up behind me with a deep sigh.

"Looks like we hit a dead end."

I nodded, feeling disappointed. I had felt so confident we were onto something here. Now, it felt like we were back to square one, even though I didn't want to admit it.

Chapter 32

Sarah Abbey had run track in high school and even gone to state, where she placed third in her junior year. It was many years ago now, but at this moment, storming outside of her prison into the street, she was suddenly so grateful her mother had pushed her not to quit running back then. She was still fast, even though it wasn't as fast as she used to be. But as the adrenalin kicked in, she was able to accelerate and get as far away as humanly possible.

As she looked behind her to make sure she wasn't being followed, she charged into an elderly lady. She forced her into the bushes next to her and made her drop the bag in her hand. The woman screamed for dear life and stared at her like she was being attacked. Seeing this, Sarah stopped, picked up the bag, and handed it to her, saying, "I am so sorry."

Sarah fumbled with the bag while the elderly woman stared at her, eyes wide and frightened. Sarah realized what she must look like as the woman pulled the bag from between her hands with a disapproving grunt.

"Are you hurt?" Sarah asked, her heart pounding in her chest, eyes glancing toward the street where she had come from, fearing to see her kidnapper show up at any moment.

You pierced a nail into their chest! That should give you some time.

The elderly woman nodded, clinging to her handbag. Sarah took off again, heading toward an intersection where she could cross the street. She sprinted along the sidewalk and reached a strip mall, where she slowed down, then merged in with the crowd of shoppers, catching her breath while zigzagging between them, blending in as best as she could without turning heads because of her dirty and torn clothes. Luckily, most people were too busy with their own quests even to notice her. A few children did, though, and pointed at her. One even laughed.

As she walked past the stores and reached another parking lot, Sarah took off running again. She spotted a park and realized she knew where she was.

"Mead Botanical Garden," she mumbled.

Sarah crossed the street and went in. She sat on a bench in the garden's amphitheater and caught her breath. Then she began wondering what to do next. Where could she possibly go? A police car drove by on the street outside the garden, and her heart sank.

If only she could go to the police.

But if she couldn't go to them, where could she turn for help? She couldn't go home to Viera. Her kidnapper had taken her from that place.

Sarah sat on the bench, contemplating what to do next as the sun began to set behind the tall trees. Suddenly, exhaustion and fatigue overpowered her. So, she put her head down—*just for one second*—and closed her eyes.

Less than a minute later, she was heavily asleep. Meanwhile, a bright red 1991 Ford Skyranger drove by outside the garden and stopped for a second by the entrance, revving the engine a few times, then decided to continue, tires screeching on the asphalt.

Part III
THREE DAYS LATER

Chapter 33

Grocery shopping with two infants wasn't the easiest thing in the world. I had Angel in a sling on my chest and Owen in his car seat inside the cart, pushing him through Publix, when I turned down the cereal aisle and saw her.

Kim!

I stared at her. She hadn't seen me yet and studied the label of a cereal box from the organic section. At first, I wondered if I should simply turn around and walk away but then thought about it again.

I'm not the one who should be ashamed of myself.

Instead, I lifted my head high, then pushed the cart down the aisle toward the cereal when she lifted her gaze and spotted me. She froze completely. Her eyes landed on Owen inside the cart.

"Hello, Kim," I said, pretending like it wasn't the most awkward encounter in the history of grocery encounters. "How are you today?"

Her eyes didn't leave Owen, and I could tell she was struggling within herself. She stood utterly paralyzed and stared at her grandchild. I remained still too and let her, hoping that seeing him would wake some kind of maternal instinct inside her.

I had asked Christine to talk to Amy's boyfriend at school and maybe find out if he knew where Amy was, but she said he had simply told her he hadn't seen her for months. We didn't believe him, of course, but were also contemplating what to do next. If Amy was hiding at his place, then we had to tread carefully. Christine said that Amy had told her that he didn't know she had a baby. She didn't even tell him that she was pregnant and ran away before it showed on her body. If she was hiding with him, it wasn't as easy as that to go there and ask her to come back. She was hurting, and it needed to be done the right way.

Meanwhile, I was drowning in diapers and barely got any sleep. Still, Owen was growing on me, and I had to admit, I was beginning to care about him a lot—almost like he was my child. I wasn't even sure I'd give him to Kim and Phil if they asked me. I wanted to make sure he ended up in a home where there was love. I'd rather live like this, getting no sleep and constantly taking care of a baby, than live knowing he was in a place where they didn't care about him, where they didn't love him.

If anyone could do it, it was me, I told myself. Matt was of another opinion, naturally. But we were just different that way.

"He's gorgeous, right?" I finally said. "He started to smile yesterday."

And you missed it. Just like you'll miss the first time he rolls over, the first time he sits by himself or pulls himself up to stand. How can you live with that?

Kim looked up at me, her eyes wide. Her lips parted like she wanted to say something, but no words came out.

"Anyway," I said as Angel started to fuss in the sling, "I should get these two home. It's feeding time."

I pushed the cart past Kim, then got down to the sugary non-organic cereal, feeling her eyes on me as I filled up the cart with Cheerios and Frosted Flakes. I sensed she was still watching me as I grabbed the cart again and pushed it further down when suddenly she spoke, "Eva Rae?"

Startled at the sound of her voice, I turned to face her. She walked closer.

"Yes?"

She swallowed. She was about to say something; then, it seemed like she regretted it.

Come on, lady, say something. Here I am, working my behind off to take care of your grandchild. At least tell me you appreciate what I'm doing. Tell me you're sorry. Something. Anything!

Her lips parted, and a sound left her mouth. "I...I..."

Yes?

Then she lowered her eyes again. "Let me know if you need anything. Like financially."

I glared at her, unable to speak a word. She was offering me money? She thought money was what her grandson needed?

Were these people for real?

I answered with a scoff, then turned away and pushed my cart to the end of the aisle. As I joined the line for the cash register, I shook my head. Owen started to wail inside the cart, and I took him in my arms while whispering in his ear that I would never let those people anywhere near him. It suddenly made a lot of sense to me that Amy had run away. She had learned from the best how to avoid responsibility.

"They don't deserve you," I whispered. "No, they don't."

Chapter 34

Lily looked in the rearview mirror at the cars behind her. She was going sixty over the bridges toward the islands after spending the day at The Avenues in Viera, shopping. As she glanced in the rearview mirror, she again got that strange feeling that someone was following her.

"You're being paranoid," she sang into the car, repeating her boyfriend Peter's words. He had been mad at her for going up to that guy at Coconuts on the Beach. Well, not mad exactly, more like surprised, he said. Why she would get in that man's face like that, he didn't understand; he said on their way home in his car.

That had made her even angrier. Was she just supposed to accept that this guy was following her? He had been everywhere lately. The café, the gym, and she was almost certain she had seen him outside of her house too, but she wasn't completely sure of that.

"Cocoa Beach is such a small town," Peter had argued. "I see the same people in many places. That doesn't mean they're following me."

"I am not paranoid," she had said, then slammed the car door shut without kissing him goodbye. She didn't want to have to deal with him at that moment. Didn't he understand that all she wanted was his support? Lily hadn't talked to him since and decided she was getting tired of him anyway. He was sloppy, smoked way too much pot, and didn't even have a job. Giving drum lessons to a couple of elementary school kids once a week wasn't exactly a real job. He still lived with his parents, for crying out loud. Meanwhile, Lily was going places with her music career and had landed a record deal recently. They weren't exactly compatible.

Her agent had told her that there would have to be sacrifices made, and Peter would probably be the first one. Lily wasn't too sad about that. She cared for him, but she didn't love him.

"Time for a change," she said to herself in the rearview mirror, smiling. She could already see her stage name in neon lights.

LIL.Y

She had put the period in between the L and the Y to give it a double meaning. It was quite clever, she believed. The thought of her bright future ahead made her turn up the radio and start to sing. She sang along to Billie Eilish's song, dreaming of becoming as big as her when the car engine suddenly went out. It didn't even sputter or make a noise; it simply died from one second to the other. The music stopped, and so did the engine. The car was still rolling as she was going down the bridge.

"What the…?"

Lily shrieked and steered the car onto the side of the road, then hit the brakes. The car came to a full stop, and she panted agitatedly while the other vehicles were rushing past her, going so fast it shook her vehicle.

She tried to start it again, but nothing happened. It was completely dead.

"Oh, no," she complained. "Not again. Please, start. I have to be at work in a few minutes, please?"

But the car remained lifeless. Lily groaned and leaned back in the seat, placing two hands in front of her face, screaming into them. It was the third time this month she'd be late for her job at the café, and they'd most certainly fire her. She couldn't catch a break, could she?

"Argh!" she moaned into the car when suddenly another car drove up behind her and stopped. Lily peeked at it in the rearview mirror, surprised at this. Had someone actually stopped to help her? Could she be that lucky? If this person had jumper cables, they might be able to revive her battery, and she would only be a little late for work. Maybe her boss, Shana, could forgive her for being a bit late if Lily told her what happened.

She opened the door and got out. She felt so uplifted and hopeful that she couldn't stop smiling. Not until a second later, at least, when she looked into the eyes of the person that had stopped.

Then, everything inside her froze to ice.

Chapter 35

T HEN:
"There are some men here to talk to you."

Lynn looked up from her papers when her secretary peeked into her office. Lynn took off her glasses as two men came up behind the secretary. It was Monday, and Lynn didn't see patients on Mondays. This was the day for paperwork, and she was lagging terribly behind.

"What is it regarding?"

"It's the...police," her secretary said, whispering the last word. "Detectives."

The two men came inside, and Lynn looked at them as they sat down. They presented themselves as Detective Fraser and Detective Harder.

"How can I help you, Detectives?" Lynn asked, puzzled.

"You have a patient that we have taken some interest in," Detective Harder said.

Lynn wrinkled her nose. This was unusual. "Okay?"

"A Jeffrey Johnson."

"I can't disclose whether or not he is a patient here. You know that."

They exchanged a look briefly before Detective Fraser continued. "We know that. But we are a little desperate here."

"Can you tell me what this is regarding?"

"His girlfriend—or rather ex-girlfriend—has been missing for quite some time now," Harder said and showed Lynn a picture of Joanna Harry, the woman Jeff had been with when he came to Lynn in the first place when they came in for couple's therapy.

"Do you know her?"

"I can't tell you that."

"Of course not. But, as I said, she has been missing for six months now, and we are frankly a little desperate to get her back."

"And how do you figure I can help?"

They exchanged another look, then Fraser said, "We know it's a little unorthodox, but we fear he might have hurt her, and well, we thought that maybe you could get him to talk about her."

"Why don't you ask him yourselves?"

"We did, but he refuses to say anything about her whereabouts. We think he's lying, naturally."

"I think if someone tells you he didn't harm her, then chances are, he didn't," Lynn said. "Innocent till proven otherwise."

Fraser sighed. "We had just hoped that maybe you could talk to him and maybe ask him about her. Maybe he'll open up to you."

Lynn sighed and pinched the bridge of her nose. "I am sorry, Detectives. I can't do that. But, as always, if I do hear anything that causes concern in any of my patients, concerns for their own or other's health, then I will make sure to get in touch."

The detectives looked at one another, disappointed. They got up.

"Thank you for your time."

They left and closed the door behind them, while Lynn just sat there, staring into thin air, unable to calm her beating heart.

Chapter 36

"I was certain that there was a connection between the murder of Tommy Carlson, Sarah Abbey's old boyfriend two and a half years ago, and her recent disappearance. It's so frustrating, and now we're back to square one."

I took the chicken out of the oven and placed it on the counter. I had asked Matt to carve it up for me. It smelled heavenly. Olivia was looking after the babies in the living room while I cooked, something that hadn't happened a lot lately. We had eaten so much pizza I could barely say the word without someone making gagging sounds. So tonight, I had made a real homecooked meal with chicken and mashed potatoes and green beans.

"But the guy was dead when it happened. He died four years ago," Matt said while finding the knife in the drawer. "And that's where it ends."

I poured the potatoes into the bowl and started to mash them, then sent him a look. "It sure hasn't ended for Sarah Abbey."

He shrugged. "Maybe you've got it all wrong from the beginning. What if she just left without a word? Didn't you say that she left her family and boyfriend without an explanation some years ago?"

I nodded while mashing and letting all my frustrations out on those poor potatoes.

"Sure. But back then, she at least called her brother to say she was all right. She told him not to look for her. That hasn't been the case this time around. As a matter of fact, she told Scott to look for her if she disappeared. She said that two months ago. She must have had a feeling it could happen. That makes me think that something awful happened to her—that she feared for her life."

"Maybe she's just nuts," Matt said and cut off a thigh, then placed it on the plate before moving on to the breast part of the chicken.

I grunted while mashing, then stopped.

"Excuse me?"

He continued to cut and wasn't looking at me.

"What kind of an argument is that? *She is just nuts?*"

He shrugged. "Some women are like that."

I lifted both my eyebrows. "Was that meant for me?"

He shrugged. "You have been a little…lately."

I stared at him. I had completely stopped mashing the potatoes. "What's that supposed to mean?"

He looked up. "How about taking in Amy and now caring for her child? Refusing to let the authorities take over?"

"That's nuts to you?" I asked, surprised.

He didn't look at me but continued to carve the chicken, putting the pieces on the plate with swift, angry movements.

"Kind of. It's not normal, at least."

"Wow."

"What?"

"Nothing. We're just farther apart than I thought."

He scoffed. "You won't even hear what I have to say. It's like I don't exist—like I don't have a say in the matter. I keep telling you it's too much for you, that you need to let go. It's not only your life that is disturbed by this. It's all of us. When is the last time you had time alone with Alex, huh? He's getting more and more loud and annoying while begging for your attention. Do you know what Christine is doing in the afternoons? Because she hasn't been coming home straight after school, I can tell you that much. I bet you haven't even noticed."

"Christine hasn't been coming home after school?" I asked, puzzled. "She's probably just been practicing with the school orchestra."

Matt scoffed again. "She stopped playing the double bass weeks ago and dropped out of the orchestra."

I let go of the masher in my hand, and it plunged into the potatoes.

"She what?"

"I told you. You have been missing out on what goes on. The kids need you, Eva Rae. And frankly, so do I. Two infants are too much."

"And just how long have you known this about Christine and not told me anything?" I asked, wiping my hands on a towel.

"Don't make this about me," Matt said, raising his voice. "Don't you dare make this about me. Not when you're out there doing only God knows what with that Scott guy. When are you going to tell me what is going on between you two? Don't you think I can sense how smitten you are with him? All I have to do is mention his name, and your entire face lights up. Don't you think that hurts me?"

I shook my head, my eyes avoiding his.

"I don't do that."

"Yes, you do, Eva Rae," he said and put the knife down on the counter. "And I am sick of it. We're about to get married, and how do you think it makes me feel, seeing the way the two of you look at one another?"

I stared into the potatoes, then grabbed the masher and continued, hoping that Matt would leave this alone.

"Hey, where are you going?" I asked when he grabbed his phone and car keys. "We're about to eat?"

He shook his head. "I'll eat at my mom's tonight."

"What? Why? I made this entire dinner so we could eat it all together. As a family."

"It'll have to be without me."

I exhaled. "Matt. Come on. There's nothing between Scott and me. I promise."

"I hear you say the words, but I don't believe them, Eva Rae," he said and opened the door.

I stepped toward him. "Matt, please. Let's talk instead. Don't leave."

But it was too late. He had already slammed the door shut, and a second later, I heard his cruiser start. Alex came running up behind me, pulling my arm.

"What are we having for dinner?"

I sighed. "Chicken."

He made a face. "Aw. I really want pizza."

"Of course, you do," I said and kissed his forehead. "But not tonight, sweetie. Tonight, we're having chicken and mashed potatoes."

"Yuck," he said, then took off toward the stairs. In the living room, the babies had both started to cry.

Chapter 37

S he waited until he was done with his sandwich. He was standing underneath the streetlamp, eating it, while his girl-friend tugged on his arm, telling him they needed to go, that they were late. Covered by the darkness of the alley she was standing in, Sarah watched him throw the remains in the trash bin next to him. As he left, she moved closer, then peeked inside the open metal bin. The sandwich was still wrapped and was lying on top of something, a box, barely touching it. She looked around, then stuck her hand in and reached for it.

So, this is what it has come to, she thought, as she stared at the spinach wrap with chipotle chicken inside it. The guy had barely taken three bites of it. Sarah broke off the end piece, then closed her eyes and bit into it.

At least it's better than going hungry.

Sarah finished the wrap and felt better. She looked up and down Park Avenue. It was so odd to be back in Winter Park again. Every-thing looked the same. The same stores and most of the same restaurants were still in the same places, yet it seemed like a strange new world.

Had she ever belonged here?

Sarah walked down the street, going past a couple of restaurants where people sat at tables outside, eating and chatting happily. A couple was holding hands across the table, looking deep into each other's eyes. How Sarah missed doing things like that, how she missed normalcy.

She walked down another block when she saw the truck and stopped, her heart suddenly racing in her chest, beating hard against her ribcage. The truck was going down Park Avenue, slowly, while approaching the place where she was standing. Sarah recognized it immediately and couldn't move.

It was a bright red 1991 Ford Skyranger convertible. The same truck that she had been taken away in on the day she was kidnapped from her home.

This is it. It's coming for me.

Seeing this, Sarah began to shake. She fought not to hyperventilate yet somehow managed to get herself turned around. Forcing herself to move, she walked up to a window, then stood completely still and stared in, turning her back to the road, acting like she was watching the exhibition in the window of the old toy store, the Tugboat & the Bird. While holding her breath, she watched the red truck in the reflection of the window as it slowly cruised by behind her.

Is it stopping? Have they seen me?

Heart throbbing in her throat, she stood as still as humanly possible so she wouldn't be seen, hoping she wouldn't be recognized.

The car slowed as it came up behind her and came almost to a stop. Seeing this, Sarah's hands shook heavily, and she felt a chill go down her neck.

Please, continue. Please, just keep going.

The truck lingered for a few seconds behind her like it was checking her out, then revved the engine a few times before it finally began moving again and disappeared down the street. Sarah breathed, relieved. She felt her heart rate come down as she stared in the direction of where it had gone. There was no doubt in her mind that this was the same truck.

I need to get out of here. I need to find a good place to hide.

124

Sarah walked with long strides, moving down Park Avenue as quickly as possible without actually running, and as she reached almost the end of it, she decided to cross it. The second she did, a set of bright headlights came to life behind her in one of the parking spaces. An engine roared to life, and seconds later, she heard tires screeching. She gasped, then turned to look as the red pick-up truck jolted toward her.

Chapter 38

My best friend Melissa came to the house the next day and took me out for lunch. She grabbed Owen in his car seat when I had parked outside of Juice 'N Java, my favorite lunch place in town. We sat at the tables outside, and Melissa went in to order us a couple of sandwiches. I also asked for a cinnamon bun. They had the best cinnamon buns here. I figured if I was being healthy and eating a spinach wrap with turkey, then I could indulge in a little sweet afterward and not feel too guilty about it.

It was all about balancing it out, right?

Melissa came back out and sat across the table from me. Angel and Owen were both heavily asleep after the car ride there. Even though it was only a few minutes, it was still enough to make them doze off. It worked every time, and it gave me a little time to breathe.

"I see you have your hands full," Melissa said and handed me my coffee. I hadn't slept much the night before since the two rascals had taken turns waking up, ganging up on me, making sure I didn't close my eyes even once. Matt slept downstairs so that he could get enough rest for work today. He had come back late from his mother's, and we hadn't had time to talk.

"You and Matt are quarreling?" Melissa asked.

I gave her a look, then sipped my coffee.

"How did you know?"

She shrugged. "I saw his clothes and a blanket on the couch downstairs, and then I could tell from your face. I've known you all my life. You don't have any secrets from me."

I lifted my eyebrows. "I'm not buying that. He called you, didn't he?"

She smiled. "All right. I did talk to him last night. He said he was upset because you insisted on keeping an extra baby at the house, plus—and I got the feeling this was what he was most upset about— you were helping Scott Benton with some case? Scott Benton, Eva Rae? Really?"

I blushed. "His girlfriend is missing. You know I can't just not try and help."

"But she's done it before," Melissa said. "Disappeared without a trace, leaving her family and friends behind."

I stared at her, mouth gaping.

"You're well informed."

"Yeah, well, Matt needed to talk last night, and I met up with him down at Coconuts. We had a beer and a chat."

Melissa, Matt, and I had been friends since preschool. Our little group also included Dawn, but we didn't see her much lately since she had moved to Merritt Island. It wasn't odd that Melissa and Matt talked and met up for a beer, even though I did feel a pinch of jealousy at this moment. Still, I would rather have him confide in her than in anyone else in the world, to be honest. Melissa was probably the one person I trusted most. And there weren't many of those around, except for my sister, Sydney, of course, the movie actress. She was busy running a shelter for trafficked girls, and usually, I would be helping her, but now, I was a baby mama.

"Don't you think you might be in a little over your head?" she asked as our sandwiches arrived, and we dug in. I took a massive bite of the spinach wrap while my eyes lingered on the cinnamon bun that was waiting next to me.

"I can do it. It's just until Amy comes back. I know she will. We just need to give her a little more time."

"That's not what I was talking about, and you know it," Melissa said.

"Then, what were you talking about?" I asked, even though I knew very well the answer to that question.

She tilted her head in that annoying way that she knew I hated. "I meant Scott. Of all the people in the world, how on earth did you end up helping him? Wasn't there a drug dealer or a child molester somewhere you could throw your compassion to?"

I chuckled. I knew Melissa and Matt both hated Scott, but they didn't know him as I did.

"He's not a bad guy," I said, trying to close the conversation here. I didn't want to talk to her about Scott anymore.

She leaned forward, her eyes growing wide. "Not a bad guy? Don't you remember high school? He was the worst. We all hated him. And he was mean to everyone, not just us—the rejects. Don't you remember how he beat up his girlfriend once, that Hannah girl, who was also homecoming queen? She said he hit her because she wanted to leave him and that he even tried to run her over with his car. That's not a good guy in my book. He's bad news, Eva Rae, and you know it."

I sighed. I had a piece of lettuce stuck between my teeth that I tried to get out by using my tongue. "We only have her word for that happening. He said she made it up because she got jealous."

"And you believe that? You?"

I shrugged again. "Sure."

"That's very unlike you."

"Listen, you don't know him the way I do," I said and washed the rest of the wrap down with my coffee.

She gave me a concerned look. "Wow, Matt really was right. I didn't believe him when he said it, but you are completely blinded by Scott. Matt said it's like he holds some sort of spell over you, making you unable to see him for what he really is—scum. What is it with you two?"

I leaned back with an exhale. I was tired of this conversation.

"It's nothing. I just felt bad for him; that's all."

She looked me deep in the eyes, then gasped lightly. "Oh, dear Lord. You two had a thing in high school, didn't you? Without any of us knowing it?"

I could feel my face turn red.

"No, you're wrong."

"Yes, yes, you did. Oh, my God, that's why you're all flushed now and why you dropped everything when he showed up."

"I am helping him find his girlfriend who is missing," I said. "There's nothing more to it than that."

She shook her head. "Nope—not buying it. But what I wonder is why he's got this hold over you. What did he do to you? Did he break your heart? Was he the one that got away? And you never could get him out of your head again, huh?"

"You're being ridiculous. Of course not. It was always Matt and me. We knew we were meant for one another."

"How did this happen without me knowing about it?" she asked, completely ignoring what I had just said. "That's what I really want to know. I thought we told each other everything."

I looked down at the table.

"We…we kept it a secret."

"You snuck around? Behind our backs? Because he was dating Hannah, oh, my. Eva Rae, he used you. Don't you see? And now, he's using you again. I bet he killed his girlfriend, and now he just wants your help to look innocent. Or even better yet, maybe he's keeping her somewhere in a basement, tormenting her so she won't leave him like Hannah did."

That made me laugh, but it sounded awkward and nervous. I grabbed the cinnamon bun and bit into it.

"You read way too many mystery novels, Melissa. I'm telling you, you've got it completely wrong. Scott is a very nice guy. I am helping him out of sympathy. And because my conscience can't stand the thought that out there somewhere, his girlfriend is in trouble. That's all. Nothing else."

She grabbed my hand in hers and squeezed it. "Just promise me you'll be careful, please? I don't trust this guy."

"I think we've established that," I said and got up from my chair. I wanted to go home now. I was getting tired of this conversation with her. As I grabbed my phone, I checked to see if I had received any messages, then realized it was the fifth time I had done this since I sat down. And it wasn't Matt I was hoping would call or text, I found out to my surprise. It was Scott.

I hadn't been in contact with Scott for several days now, and much to my astonishment, I realized that I missed him. I couldn't stop worrying about him and where he was. He had promised to stay under the radar so the police wouldn't find him, while I tried to find another angle we could use to find his girlfriend. As I carried Angel to the car and Melissa came up behind me with Owen, I realized to my regret that part of me wasn't sure I wanted to find Sarah. Because then it would be all over. Scott would have no reason to call or come to my house anymore, and we would lose contact again. I didn't want that. I liked having him around. As I said goodbye to Melissa, hugging her tightly, then waving at her, I felt my heart beating fast in my chest.

Was Melissa right? Had I lost myself in him? If so, then what did it mean? Didn't I want to marry Matt anymore?

I closed my eyes briefly, clasping my mouth. The thought was unbearable and brought tears to my eyes. What was happening to me?

I shook my head.

No, you can't think like that. You simply can't. Everything is perfect now. Don't ruin it. Why do you always have to do this to yourself? Why do you have to ruin everything good in your life?

I grabbed Angel's seat by the handle and left Owen next to the tire, right next to me, while strapping down Angel inside the car. As I pulled my head back out and reached down to grab the handle of Owen's car seat, my hand came back empty. I looked down and realized it was gone.

Owen wasn't there.

Chapter 39

Lily stared at the man approaching her, heart throbbing in her chest. It was him. She could barely understand it. It was the same guy who had been following her everywhere—the stalker.

"Are you having car trouble?" he asked, smiling, almost smirking.

"W-what are you doing here?" she asked, taking a step back as he came closer.

A thousand scenarios rushed through her mind, none of them ended well for her. Cars sped by on the bridge, and she wondered if anyone would stop and help if he attacked her. Would they even see?

"I was just passing by on the bridge when I saw you had stopped," he said, still smiling.

Lily wished he'd stop doing that. It made him even creepier. She fiddled with her phone, wondering if she could somehow call Peter without this guy noticing it. She didn't want to anger him. But Peter hadn't answered when she called earlier, right when the car died. Why would she think he'd do it now?

"Can I help?" he asked.

"Stop right there," she said and held out her hand. "Don't come any closer."

He stopped. "I didn't mean to scare you. I just wanted to help. You looked like you needed it. Did you run out of gas?"

She breathed heavily. This guy scared her so much.

"It's the battery," she said. "It has happened before."

"The battery, huh?"

"It's okay. I've already called for help. They'll be here soon," she lied. The fact was she hadn't been able to get ahold of anyone, and she didn't have any roadside assistance. She couldn't afford it. She was stuck there, and this creepy stalker was her only help.

"Oh, okay," he said. "I could give you a jump start if you need it."

"I don't." She turned her head away to avoid looking directly at him. "I don't need your help."

"It's no trouble at all. I got the cables in my trunk."

Lily stared at him. Her pulse was quickening as she contemplated taking his help. It wasn't like anyone else was coming, and she really had to get to work. If he tried anything, she had the phone in her hand and could dial nine-one-one.

"Let me just go get them," he said. "I really just want to help."

Lily thought it over for a few seconds more, then exhaled, her shoulders coming down. "All right. If it's no trouble, then…"

The man's face lit up. "It really isn't. Let me just go and get them. Give me a sec. I'll be right back."

Lily watched him go back to his car and open the trunk. She looked at her phone to see if Peter had called her back or texted her, but there was nothing. With her pulse throbbing in her throat, she watched the man pull out jumper cables from his car, then approach her. She imagined him using them to tie her up before throwing her in the trunk. As he came closer and closer, she could hear her own heartbeat.

He held up the cables.

"All right, let's do this, shall we?"

Chapter 40

"Owen?"

I said his name like I believed he'd be able to answer. Panic had started to set in as I scanned the area around me, searching for the car seat carrier with Owen inside it.

It couldn't just have vanished, could it? It had been right there, right there next to me. And now, it wasn't. I didn't understand. Melissa had put him there while I took care of Angel. I had only taken my eyes off of him for a few seconds.

Could Melissa have put him somewhere else? Or taken him? But how? She had left. I waved at her as she walked to her car. It was gone now; the car was gone from the spot where it had been.

Think, Eva Rae. Think!

"Owen?" I shrieked, then walked around the car. Inside, Angel had woken up and was fussing now. I was trying to keep the panic inside me at bay, but it was getting harder. My heart was beating so hard, it almost hurt, and I felt like screaming.

Could Melissa have taken him? I thought again. It made no sense; why would she? Yet I grabbed my phone and called her.

"Did you take Owen?"

"What do you mean?"

"The baby. The boy. Owen."

"No. I put him right next to you. You saw me do it, and then I left."

"But...but..."

"Do you mean to tell me he's not with you?" Melissa said, her voice getting loud and pitchy.

"I...I don't know," I said and placed my other hand on my head while tears of desperation sprang to my eyes. I scanned the area repeatedly, but there was no sign of the baby or the carrier.

"What do you mean you don't know, Eva Rae? Have you lost your mind?"

That was a good question. It felt like I had.

"Maybe. I don't know where he is, and I can't find him, Melissa. I can't see him anywhere."

"What are you talking about? A baby doesn't just vanish?"

I felt like screaming. "I don't know what to do, Melissa. Please, help."

"I'm turning the car around. I'll be right there. Just stay calm."

"That's easy for you to say. It's a little hard when you're missing a baby," I yelled back at her, then hung up.

I turned around, scanning the area again. There wasn't a soul in the parking lot, but a few cars were parked at the other end of it. I grabbed Angel in my arms, then walked toward them. As I did, I suddenly heard the sound of a child crying. I turned to look at the church next to the parking lot all the way to the far end.

"Owen?" I shrieked, then ran toward the building. The crying got louder, and now I recognized it as Owen's. I came up to the stairs, and that's when I saw him in his car seat, placed on the top step by the entrance to the church. His face was torn as he wailed his little heart out, but he seemed okay otherwise. I grabbed the car seat carrier just as Melissa drove up and stopped her car. She got out, and her face strained with distress.

"I found him," I said while tears rolled down my cheeks—tears of relief.

"Oh, thank God," Melissa said and clasped her chest.

She hurried up the stairs and grabbed Angel from my hands

while I reached inside the carrier and got Owen out. I held him tight to my chest, rocking him back and forth to calm him.

"How did he end up all the way over here by the church?" Melissa asked and looked toward the parking lot where my car was still parked. "It's not like he can walk on his own?"

I held his little body close to mine, then sniffed him. "I know that scent," I mumbled. "I know it. It's Amy's. She was here. She was with him."

Melissa looked up at me, eyes big and round. "Amy? The mother? You mean she was here? I thought she was missing?"

I exhaled while turning on my heel to look around me.

"I had a feeling she wasn't far away. I guess missing him got too much for her, and she had to steal a moment with him. That's the only explanation I can come up with."

Chapter 41

THEN:

She hadn't slept much the night before. Since the detectives had been to her office, Lynn had been constantly worried about Jeff. She couldn't stop thinking about Joanna and her disappearance. How could the police think Jeff had anything to do with that?

She couldn't wrap her mind around it. The Jeff she knew wouldn't harm a fly. He was both charming and charismatic. And that smile...oh, my, it was...well...to die for.

Now, she was waiting for him to enter her office, fiddling nervously with her pen. She had left the door ajar and told the secretary to tell him that he could walk straight in. She had his file ready and was staring at what she had written down the last time he was in her office.

"Hi, Doc."

She looked up, and her gaze met his. Then, her heart dropped. He was even more handsome than she remembered him. And he was wearing what looked like a brand new suit—an expensive one, it seemed.

Don't let his good looks dazzle you and blur your judgment.

"Hello, Jeffrey," she said, trying to keep the tone professional.

He sat down on the couch in front of her. He tilted his head, smiling. "You okay there, Doc?"

She tried to ease up. He wasn't supposed to sense that she had her guard up. "I'm fine, thank you. And you? How are you today? Take your time to answer."

"I'm actually doing pretty well, Doc," he said, grinning. "It's been a great week at work. A big deal went through, and I got a huge bonus. I bought myself a new Dolce & Gabbana, as you can see."

"I see that. You look very nice."

"I have to get back to work after this, and I figured you wouldn't mind me looking sharp," he said.

Oh, that smile. She couldn't liberate herself from staring at it intensely, and now he noticed. Their eyes locked for a few seconds, and she felt such a deep warmth spread inside of her. She closed her eyes to try and shake it.

"I'm glad you're doing well. And you have accepted the break-up?"

"Yes, yes, I have. I found out Alice wasn't for me anyway."

Lynn noted this on her pad. "That's good. Does this mean you're not sad about it anymore?"

"Of course, I'm still sad," he said. "I mean, I really liked her, but I found out she was just a substitute for the real deal. I was just with her because she reminded me of someone else."

Lynn looked up and blushed. His latest girlfriend had been her spitting image. Was he talking about her?

"Really?"

He nodded, rubbing his hands together. "Yes, really."

She pondered for a few seconds if she should ask more but then stopped herself. She wasn't sure she could deal with the answer.

"And Joanna?"

He grew serious. "What do you mean?"

She didn't look at him but down at her pad. "Have you managed to let her go? I remember we talked about you following her still. Have you seen her since then?"

Jeff grew silent. Lynn lifted her eyes to look at him, hoping she'd be able to read the truth on his face. He stared at her, biting his lip like he was contemplating what to say next, unsure if he could be honest.

He cleared his throat and shook his head. "It's over long ago."

"But you haven't seen her since then?"

A shadow went over his face, and his eyes grew dark. "Who have you been talking to?"

She shook her head. "I was just wondering; that's all. I know how hard it was for you to let her go."

"You've been talking to the police, haven't you? They've been here?"

"Is that important?"

"Yes, it's important," he almost yelled.

Lynn's eyes grew wide, and her pulse quickened. Jeff rose to his feet and paced in the room.

"God, I can't believe they came here to see you too."

"Sit down, Jeff, please."

He didn't. Instead, he kept pacing back and forth, making Lynn nervous.

"Jeff, please," she said. "If you and I are to talk together today, then I need you to sit back..."

"I can't believe the nerve they have," he said, stomping his foot angrily. "This is harassment. They have no right to..."

Lynn swallowed and thought about the button next to her chair, then one that alerted the front office of an emergency so they could call the cops in case a patient got aggressive. She really hoped she didn't have to use it. Jeff was the last person she wanted to have to use it on.

"Jeff..." she said, sounding firm. "Sit down, please."

He stopped pacing and stared down at her. She was suddenly acutely aware of how big he was compared to her. He looked at her, then walked closer. Lynn had her finger on the button as he hovered above her.

"Look me in the eyes, Doc. Are these the eyes of someone who could harm another human being?"

Lynn looked into his eyes, long and deep. She felt herself ease up, and her finger slowly slipped off the button. What was it about this guy that just made her melt completely?

"Do you really think I would harm her?" he asked, his voice growing soft and tender. "Me?"

Lynn smiled, then shook her head with an exhale.

"No, Jeff. I don't."

That made him smile, then he leaned forward, grabbing her face between his hands. He planted his lips on hers, and everything exploded inside of her as they shared a kiss.

Chapter 42

M att was smacking his lips as he ate the last meatball on his plate. I had made spaghetti and meatballs for dinner but didn't have much of an appetite myself. I kept staring at my future husband, wondering what was going on with me.

Was I about to make the biggest mistake of my life?

Was I in love with someone else?

I closed my eyes briefly and pinched the bridge of my nose. No, I just needed sleep; that was all. Matt was right about one thing, taking care of two infants was threatening to tear me apart.

"I'm done; can I be excused?"

Alex looked up at me with his big eyes. He had gotten close to Matt these past several months, and I knew he adored him, especially after Matt took him to work with him one day, and they walked next door to the fire station, where he got to sit in the big truck, the one with the ladder. He kept telling the fire chief that it was "on his bucket list" to sit in the big firetruck, and now he could cross that off.

We had laughed a lot at that.

Why didn't we laugh anymore?

"Sure, sweetie."

Alex smiled, left the table, took his plate out to the dishwasher, and then ran for the stairs and his room. My mom had bought him a new firetruck for his collection, and all he wanted was to play with it. It was all he talked about.

"Anyone want seconds?" I asked and smiled at my family.

Christine looked up, and our eyes met. I had scolded her for stopping bass lessons and told her that I wanted her to continue, at least finish the year. I didn't like her quitting like this for no apparent reason other than "it was a lot of work" and because she wanted to hang out with her friends downtown, which apparently was what she had been doing since she quit. The conversation hadn't ended well, and she had yelled at me that she hated me.

Nothing new there.

"No thanks, Mom. It was really good, though." Olivia rose to her feet and walked to the kitchen as well, followed by Elijah, who didn't say a word. Nor did he take his plate out, as was the custom here in our house. I had told Matt that he needed to teach his son to do as the rest of the kids did, but even Matt forgot to take his things out and just left the table to watch TV—without a word to me.

We hadn't talked at all. I simply didn't know what to say to him. Every time I opened my mouth, it felt like we ended in a fight. And with the babies always demanding me, there really wasn't time or energy for a long talk. It mostly became words yelled at one another in passing.

It wasn't good.

As they all left the table, I looked at my phone. I had been staring at it all day, wondering what Scott was up to, where he was. Why did I spend so much energy thinking about him when I had everything I needed right here?

I stared at the empty table. Everyone had left, and the dirty dishes were piling up in the kitchen.

"Guess I'll clean up then too," I mumbled and got up. I was carrying the big pot out with me when my phone suddenly vibrated on the dining table. I almost dropped the pot when I put it on the counter and ran for the phone and picked it up, panting.

"Scott?"

Chapter 43

She almost tripped when she realized that the truck was coming toward her. Sarah gasped, then leaped forward, just in time for it to miss her. It roared past her. Panting and agitated, she then turned to look and watched it come to a stop. It stayed there like it was watching her for a few seconds before it finally took off again. She watched it turn a corner, then drive down a side street, tires screeching. Heart pounding, she stared in the direction it had come from when she realized it hadn't left. It was just taking a trip around the block, and soon it peeked back out further up the one-way street.

Ready to come back.

Heart throbbing, Sarah took off running. She stormed down a side street, panting, running, gasping for air, continually looking over her shoulder. Then she spotted the bright red Ford pick-up truck turn the corner she had just left and drive down the street.

Sarah made it to the end of it, then turned right and ran into a small square that she crossed, hearing the truck roar behind her. She could hear it coming closer and closer, fast, and knew she could never outrun it. Instead, she searched for an escape, a hideout, and spotted a restaurant. She decided it was her only chance and went for it, crossing the street. The truck came roaring up behind her as she sprang for the door, and it missed her just as she opened it and fell inside.

Panting, she stared at the glass door closing behind her, then up at the two men standing above her. They were both wearing uniforms.

Police!

One bent down and looked at her. His eyes were gentle.

"Are you okay?"

She sat up, then corrected her hair, even though she knew she had to look awful right now. They probably just took her for a drunk homeless person.

"I'm sorry," she said. "I tripped."

His eyes rested on her, and his head tilted. "Say, haven't I seen you before?"

Sarah looked away. "No, no, I'm sure you haven't."

He snapped his fingers. "Yes, I have. Wait a second. I think we have a missing person's search out on you."

He grabbed his phone to look through a series of pictures. Sarah stared at him, heart throbbing. She glanced toward the door, wondering if it would open and her kidnapper would enter, or if the truck was waiting for her out there, the driver thinking she had to come back out at some point.

"No, not me."

"Yes, isn't this you?" he asked and showed her an old picture of Sarah. She knew exactly where it was taken. It was the picture of her and Scott from their vacation in Scotland last year.

Sarah shook her head.

"That's not me."

He gave her a severe look. "I think it is you. You better come with me."

The officer turned his head to address his colleague, who was getting leftover bags from the waiter.

"Jackson. I think we found Sarah Abbey."

While he looked away, Sarah saw her chance. She rose to her

feet, then rushed for the door. She hurried outside while she heard them yelling from behind her.

Soon, she could hear footsteps behind her as they tried to catch up to her, but she was fast, faster than ever. The last thing she wanted was to be taken to the station and tell them what had happened.

The consequences would be devastating. She couldn't risk it.

Chapter 44

The head of Cocoa Beach Police Department, my good friend Chief Annie, met me in the station's lobby. I had called her and told her I needed to talk to her.

We hugged. Annie gave the best hugs.

"How is the baby?" she asked as we walked in through the glass doors. They were building the new police station across the street from this one since the old one had suffered severe damage during Hurricane Irma that ravaged our area a few years earlier. The roof had never been properly repaired, and there was visible water damage on the ceiling.

"Good," I said, not mentioning the second infant in my house. I kept thinking about Amy, wondering how she had known where to find us. Had she seen us sitting outside at the café and then followed me into the parking lot just to steal a few seconds with her baby? Just to hold him? I couldn't blame her. It had to be devastating not to be able to be with him all the time. Just being away for an hour or two from Angel made my heart ache, even though I knew she was with her dad. Amy hadn't been with Owen for weeks. It had to be killing her.

If you miss him so much, why don't you just come back?

I still believed she would. At some point, it was going to be too unbearable for her, and then she'd show up. I was certain of it, but I knew how tough it was. I felt it in my own body. But I also knew how tough it was to be fifteen. She was just a child herself. And she had no help from her family.

It was rough.

"Not keeping you up at night too much, I hope?" Annie said as we entered her office, and she closed the door behind us. "You look great."

I paused. Did she just tell me I looked great? No one had complimented me for a very long time, and it almost made me cry.

I sat down. Annie folded her hands on the desk. "You came here because of that guy, Scott Benton?"

I nodded. "He called me and said you had brought him in earlier today."

Annie cleared her throat. "We did. Our patrol car drove by on Pineda Causeway, on the bridge, when they spotted two stopped vehicles. As they slowed down to ask if anyone needed help, they saw Scott Benton and a young girl, Lily Mitchell, in what appeared to be a quarrel. They stopped the patrol car and saw Scott Benton grab the girl's arm, pulling her against her will. They got out to see what was going on, and the girl screamed for their help, then ran to them as Scott Benton loosened his grip on her. She told them he was trying to kidnap her, and our officers brought him in."

I stared at her, barely blinking. Scott hadn't told me all this when he called. He had just said he was arrested on the bridge, and I had assumed her was taken in because he was a suspect in Sarah's disappearance. Hearing this story made my heart drop. What the heck was he doing?

Was I wrong about him?

"When we brought him in, we realized he was wanted by the Winter Park Police Department, suspected in the disappearance of his girlfriend."

"Sarah Abbey," I said

"Oh, so, you know."

I sighed. "Yes. I've been trying to help him find her, but we ran out of clues."

Annie nodded. "I had a feeling it was something like that. How do you know this guy?"

"High school," I said. "Let's just leave it at that."

"Ah, I see. Well, the two of you are in luck today."

I lifted my gaze to meet hers.

"What do you mean?"

"I just got off the phone with Winter Park, and they told me he was no longer a suspect."

"Really?"

She nodded. "Yes. Sarah Abbey was spotted by a couple of colleagues in a restaurant in Winter Park a few hours ago. She's alive and well. Not very interested in talking to the police since she took off running, but your friend is off the hook. For now, at least."

I leaned back in the chair, feeling confused. Had Matt been right, then? Had Sarah just left once again?

"I'll be…"

"Yes, guess your friend lucked out. Our girl, Lily Mitchell, isn't going to press charges against Scott Benton as long as she never sees him again, so he's being released tonight. You can take him with you when you leave."

Chapter 45

THEN:

"I'll have the tuna salad on rye."

Lynn looked at Stan sitting across from her. He was still looking through the menu as always, taking forever to decide, and then when he did, he'd always end up getting jealous of her food, and they'd end up sharing.

"I'll grab the Angus burger," he said and handed the waitress the menu. "Medium rare and with a side of cheese fries."

"Sure. Anything else?" the waitress asked.

They both shook their heads, and she left. Lynn folded her hands and leaned her elbows on the table. She looked at her boyfriend, staring him deep in the eyes. Things between them had been bad lately, or maybe not that bad, just different. It was like they didn't quite click the way they used to. She was thinking a lot about Jeff, and that, of course, had something to do with it. She wasn't really present anymore, and Stan was beginning to notice.

"So, what's going on?" he asked with a light shrug. "Anything new at the job?"

He asked this even though he knew she couldn't tell him

anything about her work, except for the rare occasion when one of the ladies at the front desk quit or had the flu.

She shook her head and leaned her chin on her hands. "Not really. Just same old, same old. And you? How are things at the dean's office?"

"They're good, as usual. Dean O'Conner drives me nuts and is just too old for his position, in my opinion. I mean, we need new, fresh eyes on what to do with the campus if we're ever to make any progress. I've come up with many new suggestions, but he doesn't care. If it ain't broken, then why fix it, right?"

"Well, that was always O'Conner's approach, even when he was younger, I have heard. That's why they like him so much. He hasn't changed anything in thirty years."

"And that's what's getting to me. I work with international students registered at the Department of Medicine, right? There are over nine hundred people. I manage their academic records, follow up on examination periods, register and review their grades, and solve daily requests. That is work volume enough for at least two people, not just one. I love working with the students and helping them with their daily issues, but there is only one of me. And I have been asking for help for years, and they keep expanding the program, which means more students for me to help. But he still..."

Lynn nodded but wasn't listening anymore. She wasn't even looking at her boyfriend anymore as he went on his usual rant about his job. Something else had caught her interest—or someone. Behind Stan, a young man had entered and was now sitting right behind them, ordering a coffee. He was simply sitting there, staring at her intently, while sipping his cup, smiling from ear to ear.

Jeff.

Lynn tried to focus on what her boyfriend was talking about, but she simply couldn't. She couldn't take her eyes off of Jeff sitting right behind him, and their eyes remained locked. Lynn felt completely pulled into his like she had no will of her own anymore.

This is not good, she told herself, yet still didn't stop and look away. *This is not good at all.*

"So, next thing I know, O'Conner is standing right behind me as

I say this," Stan said and laughed loudly. "Boy, that was embarrassing."

Lynn chuckled to let him know she was listening, even though she wasn't. All that was in her mind right now was her and Jeff. It was like no one else existed. He was just sitting there, not saying or doing anything except drinking his coffee, staring at her, and it made her lose herself altogether.

You can't do this. You can't fall for him. He's your patient.

Lynn finally broke the spell as the waitress brought their food, and she looked down at her tuna salad sandwich. She smiled at the girl, then took the first bite. As she once again lifted her gaze to look behind her boyfriend, she realized Jeff was no longer there. He was gone, and all that was left behind was his empty coffee cup on the table.

Lynn swallowed her bite and washed it down with Perrier sparkling water, feeling her heart race in her chest. What was it about him that attracted her to him so much yet made her feel creeped out at the same time?

What on earth had she gotten herself into?

Chapter 46

"I'm gonna need a heck of an explanation here, Scott. It better be good."

We had just gotten into my minivan when I turned to look at him. It had gotten dark out, and I planned to take him to his car, but it had been taken to impound, they told me. Now, I just wanted to take him to a bus stop and tell him to get lost. But at this moment, I wasn't sure I even wanted to take him anywhere—not until I knew more. I felt so betrayed and lost. Still, there was a part of me that wanted to give him the benefit of the doubt. His sweet eyes kept lingering on me, and I couldn't shake the feelings I had for him, even though I was trying so hard not to give them any attention. They refused to be pushed away, and it was driving me nuts.

Scott looked down at his hands, then shook his head slowly.

"I was only trying to help. I was driving across the bridge when I saw her. Her car had broken down, and I decided to stop and help. She said it was her battery, so I found my jumper cables in the trunk and tried to get it back to life. But as we tried over and over again, it didn't work. The battery remained dead."

I nodded, biting my lip. That didn't sound too awful. "Okay, so you helped her out, but what about what the officers saw? Why did you grab her arm? Why did she say that you were about to kidnap her?"

Scott's eyes grew wide. He turned to look at me, a look of dismay on his face. "The girl is insane. I told her I could give her a lift to town, and she refused. She said she would rather stand out there in the darkness. Her phone had died while we were working on the battery, so she couldn't call for help. I told her it was too dangerous and that I wasn't leaving her there. I mean, what should I have done? I couldn't live with myself if anything happened to her after I left. So, yes, I argued with her, but she wouldn't listen to me. She kept yelling at me, telling me just to leave, so yes, I grabbed her arm and said I'd take her home, but I wasn't even pulling her. Then, when the police came, she kept ranting on and on about how I was trying to kidnap her, and she screamed at them for help. So, of course, they took me in. But I swear, Eva Rae, the girl was just crazy and wouldn't listen to reason."

He was getting agitated as he spoke, and his nostrils flared slightly. I watched his face, trying to figure out if I believed him or not. First, there had been Hannah, who claimed he hit her and tried to run her over in his car, then there was Sarah Abbey, who had fallen down the stairs or maybe been pushed. Were they all just coincidences? If so, it was very unfortunate, and it was hard for me to believe him. But then again, there were those eyes that he looked at me with and that cute smile that I couldn't ignore. I had been so madly in love with him back then, and now, I was staring at that same face once again, unable to see any fault with the person behind it.

"I swear, Eva Rae. I was only trying to help her."

I sighed and started up the minivan.

"All right. Where do I take you now? Where are you staying?"

He exhaled. "I have sort of been sleeping in my car."

I felt like screaming. "You don't have anywhere to go?"

"I guess I could go home now that the police won't be looking for me anymore."

I looked at the clock.

"It's late. All right. I'll take you to Viera. I just need to text Matt and let him know I won't be home until much later."

"You're so good to me," he said. "Thank you. I really appreciate it."

"Well, don't make me regret it," I said and took a turn out of the police station's parking lot. I looked at him again as the minivan drove into A1A. "I mean it, Scott. Please, don't make a fool of me."

He lifted both his hands resignedly.

"I won't. I promise."

"All right. Now, tomorrow, we'll reach out to all of Sarah's family to hear if she's been in contact with them. Maybe it could be all over tomorrow, and you can be reunited with her back home. Then we can all go back to our normal lives. Wouldn't that be something?"

Chapter 47

It looked exactly the same as it had three years ago—the small house in the middle of a big empty lot. The house wasn't much, but it had the cutest wooden wrap-around porch, and Sarah remembered sitting there on endless nights with her brother, talking about their futures or crushes. Her brother was older than her by six years and always felt protective of her and who she dated. He had moved away from their parents long before she did, and she'd come and visit him as a teenager, just to get away from their parents. Only he understood what she went through. Only he ever understood her. And now, he was going to do it again.

Sarah walked up to the porch and stood by the front door for a few minutes, gathering her courage. She looked at her bare feet. She had so many scratches and was bleeding from running barefoot across town. Her arm was hurting from a fall, and her entire body ached.

And she felt so tired, so incredibly tired.

Sarah opened the screen door and knocked. She held her breath for a few heartbeats when she heard movement on the other side, and the door opened.

The sight of her brother's face made her smile nervously. He stared at her for a few seconds like he didn't recognize her, or maybe he didn't believe his own eyes. Then, he burst into a loud, happy shriek.

"Sis? Is it really you?"

Sarah nodded, feeling a pinch deep in her stomach. She had missed him more than she knew.

"It's really you? Really? Wuhuuu," he said as he grabbed Sarah around the waist and lifted her in the air.

She couldn't stop laughing. He spun her around, eyes tearing up.

"You're back? You're back?"

She nodded, biting her lip. She had thought long and hard on what to tell him, how to explain where she had been because he would undoubtedly have questions—and a lot of them. She had no clue how to avoid having to answer any of them. But she'd have to find something to say without involving her brother in all that had happened. He couldn't know.

Her brother put her down again and held the door open for her. "Come on in. I have some leftover pizza from earlier tonight if you're hungry. Are you hungry? You look hungry."

She walked inside and felt tears filling her eyes. It had been so long since she had last been in his living room. She had missed it more than she wanted to admit. She had missed her brother more than she had been willing to realize.

He used to be her everything.

"I'm starving, actually," she said, gazing toward the big pizza box on the table in front of the TV that was still running. Her brother shut it off, then handed her the box.

"Here, knock yourself out."

She grabbed a slice and started to eat while still standing. Her brother watched her closely, his eyes scrutinizing her, especially her dirty, bloody feet.

"Say, what happened to you?" he asked as she reached for the second piece. She bit into the cheese and filled her mouth, eating the heavenly bites, savoring them. Who would have thought that pizza could taste this good?

"Sis?"

She chewed, avoiding his eyes.

"Sis? Did someone try to hurt you? You look awful."

Sarah swallowed the bite, then looked at him. "Can I borrow a bed? I'm exhausted."

He nodded, eyes deep with concern. "Of course. Stay in the spare room as long as you need to. We'll talk in the morning then."

She smiled, then kissed his cheek, thinking a good night's sleep would give her a chance to come up with a good enough lie.

Chapter 48

"You're telling me you're going to help him again tomorrow?"

Matt sat on the bed; his eyes were dark and angry as he looked at me. I told him everything that had happened and that I needed him to take care of the kids the next day while I went to Winter Park.

"Are you insane? Have you completely lost it?" he asked.

I was getting undressed and took off my shirt, then threw it in the hamper. "No, Matt. I have not gone insane. I promised to help him find his girlfriend, and now we have a chance at doing so."

Matt shook his head in disbelief. He scoffed. "But if she's not in trouble, what's the point?"

I gave him an angry look. It felt like we had the same argument repeatedly, and it was tiresome.

"What is that supposed to mean?"

"Why does he need your help at all? I could remotely understand it when you thought something had happened to her, that she had been kidnapped or maybe even killed. That, I could understand. But now? Police officers saw her in a restaurant. It doesn't sound like a crime has been committed at all."

"We don't know that. I've been searching for this girl for weeks; I want to help Scott find her and make sure she's okay. See it with my own eyes. People don't just disappear for no reason. She could still be in trouble."

"Okay, how about this?" Matt said and sat on his knees. "Maybe she just doesn't want to be with Scott anymore. Have you thought about that? What if she just left him?"

"She would have left a note or something, or at least called. You don't just leave without a word."

"What if he was abusive and she left to get away from him, and now you've led him directly to her? How's that for a theory, huh? I mean, after what you told me about that girl on the bridge, I am sorry, I don't buy that excuse even for a second."

I exhaled. Part of me worried that Matt was right, but I didn't want to let him know that. I trusted Scott and believed him.

"Her boyfriend was murdered," I said, trying to cut him off. "She feared for her life. She told Scott to look for her if she ever went missing. That sounds like someone worried something might happen to her. I need to see for myself that she's all right and hear it from her own mouth. Can't you give me that?"

"You want me to ruin my only day off this week? I'm exhausted from work and the lack of sleep. And now you want me to take care of two babies all day long?"

"I do it every day," I said, almost hissing. "Chances are, it won't even be the entire day, just a few hours. I think you can manage that."

I opened the drawer and took out my PJs, then slammed it shut angrily. I got dressed, then walked to the bathroom to brush my teeth. When I returned, Matt's side of the bed was empty, and he had taken his pillow and blanket with him to the living room downstairs.

Chapter 49

S arah slept like a rock—the best she had in many weeks. When she finally woke up, it was with a loud gasp, and her heart was beating hard in her chest. She shot her eyes open and stared into the ceiling, trying to figure out where she was until it finally sank in that she was actually out of the small room. She wasn't chained to the wall anymore, and she wasn't sleeping on a bench in the park either, worrying they'd come for her.

She was safe.

Sarah sat upright, then placed her feet on the floor. The house was so quiet, and she wondered what time it was. She was suddenly so grateful that her brother had never married or had children. Her brother was gay, but not openly, and Sarah knew very little of his love life, even before she left.

She didn't like that he was so alone. It made her sad.

Sarah rose to her feet, walked to the kitchen, and got herself a glass of water. There was a note on the counter. It was from her brother, telling her he had left for work and would be back later in the day.

MAKE YOURSELF AT HOME

Sarah felt a tear escape the corner of her eye. It was so typical of him to welcome her with open arms, even though she had been gone for three years without a word. He hadn't even yelled at her or scolded her for leaving.

But he was going to demand answers to his questions, and she still didn't know how to do that.

Sarah started the coffeemaker and made a pot, then walked to the bathroom with a pair of scissors in her hand. She stood in front of the mirror and cut off big locks of her hair, letting them fall into the sink below. When she was done, she took a long shower. The sensation of water trickling over her body, washing away the dirt and old, dried-up sweat and blood was beyond satisfying. It was heavenly.

Sarah scrubbed her dirty skin and watched the brown water get washed down the drain, mixed with her dried-up blood. Then she examined herself. She still had some bruises on her arms and back from when she had been dragged into that room and locked up. Her wrists were also quite bruised from the chains—but nothing too severe, nothing that wouldn't go away over time.

Sarah stopped the water and got out of the shower, thinking about the day her kidnapper came for her, then shivered. She knew they wouldn't stop here. They were looking for her out there, and at some point, they would realize where she was. It wasn't the most secretive hideout, her brother's place.

And by staying here, she had put her brother's life in danger too.

The realization felt excruciating. But her brother's house was the only one she could think of when trying to find a hiding place. She hoped her kidnapper wouldn't know where he lived.

Sarah went to her brother's closet and found some clothes that were way too big for her, but with a belt, she could keep the jeans up, and if she rolled the legs up, it didn't look too shabby. It was better than the dirty rags she had been in for weeks in that hellhole and while staying in the streets.

She walked back to the kitchen, poured herself some coffee from the pot she just made, grabbed some cereal from the cabinet, and poured milk on top. Who knew cereal could taste like this? She thought to herself after the first spoonful. She sat in the living room while eating, trying to kill that deep hunger inside of her. Slowly, she was beginning to feel like a human again, something she had longed for.

While she ate, enjoying her freedom, she heard a car drive up the street outside and peeked out nervously between the curtains. She felt her heart rate go up rapidly as she watched a car approach. Her hand holding the curtain began to shake violently when she was suddenly reminded of the day she had been abducted from her own home.

When the car came to a stop outside, she could no longer breathe. She let go of the curtain and stormed into her brother's bedroom, where she knew he kept a gun under the bed.

Chapter 50

THEN:

She took a deep breath, then checked her make-up before telling her secretary to let him in. Jeff stormed through the door and shut it behind him. He rushed to the couch and sat down. His hair was a mess, his shirt unusually wrinkled. His cheeks were blushing, and his eyes almost manic.

"Doc," he said with a deep exhale. "I am so glad to see you again. I've missed you like crazy."

Lynn smiled and nodded, trying to hide how much it flattered her when he said stuff like that.

"How are you today?"

He sniffled, his eyes still lingering on her. "How am I? How am I?"

She smiled. "Yes, Jeff. How has your week been?"

"Awful, that's how. Simply awful."

"Okay. And why is that?"

He stared at her, mouth slightly open. "Are you seriously asking me this? You know why."

"Do I? Maybe you should explain it to me."

He ran a hand through his hair a couple of times. "I…I can't stop thinking about you. Ever since we… You're all that's on my mind, constantly, every second of the day. It's like I'm obsessed."

Lynn stared at him, suppressing a smile. "Really? Tell me more, please. Can you give me some examples?"

"I wake up in the middle of the night and think of you. I can't eat; my stomach is in knots constantly. I go on Instagram many times a day, scrolling through your account, looking at your pictures. I look at them when I…pleasure myself and…"

"Okay, okay," Lynn said. "I get the idea. Jeff, now we talked about…"

He leaned forward and grabbed her hand in his. The movement was so swift she barely had time to react.

"I can't stand being without you, Doc. You're everything there is. It's maddening. Did you read any of my emails I sent this week? You didn't answer any of them."

"I read every word," she said, looking down at her notepad. "And I do appreciate you taking your time to write to me. I just haven't had the time to write back."

His eyes eased up as he looked into hers. "I thought there was an explanation. It was driving me nuts. I kept wondering if you didn't like me anymore. I was so scared you'd leave me."

Lynn scoffed. "I'm not going anywhere, Jeff."

His shoulders came down, and he leaned back on the couch. "I am so glad to hear that, Doc. I was so worried…"

"It's those abandonment issues. We talked about those, remember?"

He nodded. "They do drive me nuts. It was just after I saw you in that restaurant and watched you, and you didn't look at me the way you usually do, so I got scared, and I've been obsessing over that ever since, fearing you'd tell me you couldn't see me again."

She lifted her gaze and met his across the room.

"I would never do that, Jeff. Ever. You're my favorite patient. I look forward to you coming every week."

He smiled and sighed. "I am so glad to hear that, Doc. Do you think we can kiss again? Because I really enjoyed that. It made me so happy; you wouldn't believe it."

Lynn sighed and took off her glasses. She looked into his eyes, then tilted her head.

"All right. But just one kiss."

Chapter 51

Matt agreed to take care of the kids, even though it wasn't willingly. We fought about it all morning, and I ended up hurrying out the door, coffee in my thermos. I didn't even say a proper goodbye to Angel and Owen. I just slammed the door shut, then hurried to my minivan and drove out to pick up Scott in Viera. I was still fuming with anger as he approached the car. His smile was charming when he got in, and I felt my anger melt away instantly.

That's the effect he had on me.

Part of me wondered if I had just been angry all morning because of Matt or if it was really because I knew that today I would most likely lose Scott if we found Sarah, as was the mission. He would be happy and take her home with him, and I would probably never see him again. It wasn't a pleasant thought. No part of it felt good. If it was true that I was really angry about losing Scott, then what did that mean for Matt and me? Was it silly of us to get married if I found myself so easily attracted to another man?

"You want a protein bar?" he asked and held one out for me. I had already eaten cereal, standing up while yelling at Matt, so I wasn't exactly hungry. Still, I took one and ate it, then washed it down with my coffee.

As we made it up on the highway, I felt myself finally ease up. I was acting insane. It had to be the hormones from breastfeeding. They made me do and think stupid things—that had to be it.

I turned up the music loud and decided to leave all the anger and resentment behind me. I'd have to deal with Matt later.

After about an hour's drive, we arrived in the small neighborhood in the south end of Winter Park, not far from the Mead Botanical garden. I had been there with Matt a few months earlier and was reminded of a wonderful afternoon marveling at the hundreds of rare plant species—back when things were a little less complicated—before the two infants came into our lives. I had to admit, I thought to myself as I drove up the narrow street toward the address in my GPS, that it was a lot taking in an extra child, and I couldn't blame Matt for being upset about it. And then there was the matter of Scott on top of it. Matt could probably sense how I was confused about my feelings and was distancing myself from him.

"I think it's that house up there on the small hill," I said and pointed ahead of me on Howell Branch Road. I drove up the driveway and parked the car in front of a small house with a wooden wrap-around porch. It was set back on an unusually big lot for being this close to Orlando. The yard was well maintained, and that was quite the accomplishment in Florida.

We got out and walked up the driveway toward the front porch. I smiled at Scott and was wondering if he was excited or nervous.

"Now, remember, we don't know if she has come to him," I said. "She could also have gone to her parents' place."

"Yeah, except she was never close with her parents," Scott said. "She might have lied about a lot, but I don't think that was untrue. She always spoke so lovingly about her brother the few times we talked about her family. He was her rock."

I nodded, feeling convinced. If Sarah really was here in Winter Park, it was very plausible that she'd seek out the one person who meant something to her.

"It doesn't look like anyone is home," Scott said, looking at the empty driveway. "Maybe we should have called first?"

I shook my head. "If Sarah is hiding, then she would have asked him not to tell anyone she was here."

"You think she's hiding?"

I nodded. "Chief Annie told me she ran away from the police when they approached her. My guess is she fears for her life, and for some reason, she doesn't want the police involved..."

I paused mid-sentence when the door to the house swung open, and a woman stepped out on the porch. She looked down at where we had stopped, the gun in her hand pointed at us.

Chapter 52

"S-Sarah?"

Scott froze in place and stared at the woman standing on the porch. I had only seen pictures of her and had to admit she didn't look much like them anymore—at least not from where I was standing. She had lost a lot of weight, and her hair was now short.

"Sarah?" he repeated.

She didn't answer. She stood at the top of the stairs, staring down at us, still pointing the gun but mostly at Scott. Her hands holding it were shaking heavily, and I saw deep fear in her eyes.

"Sarah, we've been looking for you," I said and stepped forward. "For quite some time. Are you okay?"

She didn't look at me, only at Scott, her nostrils flaring.

"Stay back," she said. "Don't come any closer."

Yet, Scott did. He took another step forward, and that made her cock the gun.

"Come any closer, and I *will* shoot you."

He stopped and lifted his hands, turning the palms toward her, a look of confusion on his face.

"But...but Sarah...?"

She shook her head.

"Don't...don't..."

"We're just so happy to see you, Sarah," I said. "We've been looking everywhere for you, thinking something bad happened to you, and..."

"I need you to go," Sarah almost hissed. "Both of you."

"But..."

"GO!"

She yelled the last part and pointed the gun at Scott.

"Get out of here, now!"

I grabbed Scott by the arm and pulled him away. We hurried out to the minivan and got in, and as we drove off, Sarah fired a shot. It didn't hit anything, luckily, but it made me speed up and go down the road so fast that we almost skidded sideways into the bushes as I turned at the end of it.

"What the heck was that about?" I yelled at Scott as we were far enough out of sight. I turned to look at him, fuming.

"I...I don't know," Scott said. "I don't understand any of this."

"She didn't exactly look like she was deeply in love with you, Scott. Or have you been lying about that too?"

He shook his head. "N-no. I don't understand what's happening. I swear to God; I don't understand, Eva Rae."

I stepped on the accelerator and rushed us out of town and onto the highway. I wanted to go home now. I needed to get away from this, as far away as possible, and forget everything about this. Matt had been right. I didn't need this drama in my life.

"There's something you're not telling me, Scott. It has been going on through all of this. I try to help you, and then little by little, all these secrets are revealed, and I don't know what to think. That girl was afraid of you, Scott. I could see it in her eyes. Why was she scared of you? Why didn't she want to see you?"

"I swear, Eva Rae, I am as clueless as you. You have to believe me."

"Yeah, well, I feel like I've heard that a little too much lately. We're done here, Scott. I'm gonna take you home to Viera now. I don't want to see you again. This is it for me. I'm out."

Part IV

ONE WEEK LATER

Chapter 53

A ngel and Owen were finally asleep, so I grabbed my laptop and walked into my bedroom. In there, I found Matt sitting on the bed, watching a show on the TV on the wall. He gave me an annoyed look, and I closed the door and continued on my way. Things hadn't exactly been good between us lately, and we pretty much avoided one another as much as humanly possible in our small house. The girls were fighting in their room, and Alex played loudly in his room while Elijah sat with his headphones on, watching something on his iPad. Downstairs, my dad and my brother, Adam, were in the middle of some discussion while my grandmother was in the kitchen, cooking something that smelled delicious while listening to Joni Mitchell on the Alexa.

My family had been here for three days now, and even though I enjoyed being with them, I was kind of tired of a crowded house. They hadn't told me how long they were planning on staying, and I didn't like to ask. I didn't want them to think I didn't like having them here.

"You want a sandwich?" my grandmother asked. "There are still a few hours till dinner."

"No, thanks," I said, smiling. My grandmother was the only one who was not on my case about losing weight these days. "I'm good. Just trying to find a quiet spot to check my email."

That made my grandmother laugh, throwing back her head with her silver ponytail. Her voice was hoarse and rough, probably from the many years of smoking. She drove here on her motorcycle and slept on the couch in the living room, along with my dad, David, and my half-brother, Adam. Not too bad for a woman who was eighty-two. They all lived together in her house on Amelia Island, only a few hours from us, but we didn't get to see one another much, so I was actually happy to have them here. Our sister Sydney would come over for dinner later; she had promised. I wanted us together, all of us as much as humanly possible, but Sydney had been so busy at the shelter, she hadn't been able to come yet. I knew Sydney was just lying to me. She had bigger issues than me about seeing our father again. She grew up with him in London after he kidnapped her when I was five, and she was seven in a Walmart. We grew up apart because of this, and she had never quite been able to forgive him for that. It was hard for me as well, but somehow, it had been slightly easier. I don't know why—maybe because I knew how easy it was to make a mess of your life. Perhaps because I grew up with our mother, who was cold and distant, and I had always longed for a parent who was different and finally found it in my father. Plus, there was no doubt that I was the one who took after him and our grandmother, not Sydney. He was messy and surrounded by constant chaos.

Just like me.

"I think I'll go in the garage," I said and pointed at the door.

That made my grandmother laugh again—a laugh that soon turned into a rough cough. I smiled and wondered how long we would still have her around. I hoped it was many years more. I wanted to get to know her better.

Barely had I opened the door to the garage before there was a knock on our front door. I walked to open it, then froze to ice as I did.

Outside stood a woman in yoga pants and a pink running top.

"K-Kim?"

"Can I see him?" she asked, tears springing to her eyes. "I really want to see him."

Chapter 54

Lily couldn't get her arms down. She had just hung up with her agent, who told her she would go on tour as soon as her album was released. The record company was so impressed with her work that they wanted to roll out the big **PR** machine and make a star of her. She had everything, they told her. The voice, the right music, and she was commercial, which her agent said meant she was pretty.

Now, she was standing in her living room, holding the phone in her hands, still staring at the display, heart thumping happily in her chest, unable to know whether to scream in joy or dance around or maybe cry.

She felt like doing all of it at once.

"They like it; they really like it," she said into the room that suddenly felt too empty. She realized she had no one to share the good news with. She was all alone.

What about Peter? You could call him and let him know?

She thought it over and then found him in her contacts, but she regretted it as she was about to press call. She had broken up with him because she didn't want him to hold her back. If she brought him into her life again, she would end up hurting him. She wouldn't be able to bear that. Breaking up with him was hard enough as it was. Seeing those sweet eyes grow teary had just about crushed her heart.

No, she couldn't let him think he had a chance with her. It would destroy him all over again.

Lily put the phone down, then went to look inside the fridge. Did she have any champagne or even just a bottle of wine?

Nope. Not even a beer.

Lily closed the door to the fridge again, then grabbed her keys and walked outside. She could buy a bottle of champagne at Publix and then celebrate on her own. She didn't need anyone here with her—this was her victory anyway. She did this on her own.

My way.

Lily walked out on the porch with her purse in her hand. The screen door slammed shut behind her, and she took two steps down when she suddenly paused, frozen in motion. Her eyes had fallen on something across the street from her, and it made her heart stop.

It was him.

He was sitting inside his car, staring at her.

Are those binoculars in his hands?

"What in the...?"

Lily felt the rage rise inside of her but didn't exactly know what to do. She couldn't believe he had come back. What a nerve this guy had. Had he learned nothing from the last time? She had told the police she didn't want to press charges against him, mostly because she didn't want to go through the trouble, and she didn't want her name involved in anything, not now when she was on the verge of her big breakthrough as a singer.

The man across the street now realized she had seen him and started the engine. He drove off, but not fast enough. She was still able to take a series of pictures of his car and the license plate as it left her street.

Then, she called the police.

Chapter 55

I took Kim to the nursery, where both babies were still sleeping. Under different circumstances, I would never have taken Owen up from his bed since I believed it was important to respect a child's sleep, but I did it this time, for Kim's sake. And for Owen's. She was showing a genuine interest in the child, and I had longed for that.

I walked out of the nursery with him in my arms, and we took him to our bedroom. Matt was still watching a movie in there, but when I told him what was going on and that Owen's grandmother had come, he turned the TV off and left.

I sat on the bed with Owen, and Kim sat next to me. She exhaled and bit her lip, probably to push back tears. She seemed different somehow, more emotional.

"He's adorable, right?" I said and held him so she could see him better. She leaned in over my shoulder and looked at his face closely.

"He…he looks…" she trailed off, and her shoulders slumped.

I gave her a look. "Do you want to hold him?"

She shook her head. "Oh, no, no. I really can't."

I didn't listen to her protests. I simply handed her the baby and put him in her arms. She mumbled something yet took him anyway, and now, she was sitting with him in her arms.

"What's going on, Kim?" I asked.

She looked at the baby in her arms with tears in her eyes and didn't give me the time of day.

"What do you mean?"

"A few weeks ago, you didn't even want to know of him."

She shrugged. "And?"

"And now, you suddenly changed your mind and want to see him?" I asked. "Has something happened?"

She shook her head. "No. Nothing. Can you maybe take a picture of me with him? Here, use my phone."

She handed me her phone and opened it for me. I took a couple of snapshots, and she smiled, holding him up for the camera. I felt more confused than ever. What had suddenly changed?

I was about to shut off the phone when I accidentally saw another photo taken recently and paused. I looked up at her.

"This picture, taken in front of the church. It was you? You took Owen that day in the parking lot?" I showed her the picture of Owen in his car seat carrier on her phone.

Kim blushed, her cheeks turning completely red.

"I...I...no."

I lifted my eyebrows. "Kim. I have the picture right here. Why would you do something like that? I thought he had been kidnapped."

She looked at me, visibly embarrassed. "I...I'm sorry. I just wanted to see him for a second and hold him and take a picture of him for...and then I panicked. I didn't want you to see me."

I shook my head in disbelief. Was this woman for real? "So, you put him on the steps and ran? Who does that?"

She shook her head with a *tsk*. "You found him, didn't you?"

"Why didn't you just come and ask me if you could hold him?"

"Well, after the last time in Publix, I wasn't sure you'd let me. Besides, I just wanted to take his picture, so..."

She paused, and I sent her a glare.

"So, what, Kim?"

She shook her head and handed me back the baby. "I should get going now. It was wrong of me to come."

She started to walk toward the door. "She's with you… Isn't she? Amy? You know where she is, right? The picture was for her, so she could see how big he had gotten. And now, you wanted a new one today so she could keep track of him and know that he's doing okay."

Kim's eyes hit the carpet. She shook her head, then opened the door. "I…I need to go. Thank you for letting me see him."

And with that, she closed the door and left. I sat back, holding Owen, unable to figure out what the heck just happened and what to make of it. These people made no sense to me. None at all.

I didn't get to finish the thought before my phone vibrated in my pocket.

Chapter 56

Bryan dropped the silverware onto the plate with a loud sound. Sarah jumped and looked at him, gun still in her hand, one eye remaining on the window.

"It's driving me insane," he said.

"What is?"

He threw his arms out. "This. You."

She turned her head briefly and looked at him before her eyes returned to look out the window at the street outside.

"What do you mean?"

"I can't stand this. You, sitting there by the window, day and night, watching for whatever it is you fear might come. You still haven't told me what happened to you."

Sarah lowered her head and studied the gun in her hand. When she was a child, her dad had taught her to shoot. She had hated it back then, but today, she was glad she knew how to defend herself. No one was going to sneak up on her and live to tell about it. Never again.

"I can't tell you. I'm sorry."

"Why not? Don't you think I deserve to know? You come here all bruised up, blood smeared on your skin, dirty like you've been living in a mudhole for months. You're scared as heck and sit by the window constantly as if you're expecting someone to come driving up to the house to attack you. Why won't you tell me anything? Every time I ask even the simplest question, you simply ignore it or answer something that doesn't tell me anything."

She exhaled. He was right—she owed him an explanation. She couldn't keep this up.

"What do you want to know?"

"Where were you? You were gone for weeks, and no one knew where to find you," he said.

"I don't know where I was," she said. "That's the problem."

A car drove up in the street outside, and she lifted the gun, keeping it ready. The headlights shone in the darkness, and Sarah couldn't tell what type of car it was.

"Okay, so tell me why you're guarding the house. Is someone looking for you? Are you in trouble?"

"I can't tell you that."

The car came closer, and Sarah held her breath as it slowed. Could this be it? Had they found her? She cocked the gun and heard her brother sigh deeply behind her.

"What *can* you tell me, huh?"

He got up and walked to the window, pulled the curtain aside, then scoffed. "That is the Thomasons' car. They're my next-door neighbors. You ought to recognize them by now," he said. "You've watched them come and go for days now."

"It's hard to see in the darkness," Sarah said. "All the cars look the same, and I'm not taking any chances."

Bryan grabbed her by the shoulders and knelt in front of her. "Just tell me, Sarah. What happened to you?"

She looked into his eyes and felt a pinch of guilt. Bryan had been so worried about her; she knew he had. And he probably still was.

"I...I was taken," she said, already regretting having said it as the words left her lips. "I was kept somewhere..."

His eyes grew wide. "You were kidnapped? By who? Did you know this person?"

She exhaled again, then shook her head slowly.

"I can't tell you. I am sorry."

He rose to his feet, throwing out his arms in frustration. "Why not? We could go to the police and tell them everything. Then you wouldn't have to live in fear like this."

Sarah shook her head, tears springing to her eyes. She couldn't stand all these questions anymore or the way her brother looked at her. She couldn't stand any of this anymore.

"I just can't, okay?" she almost yelled.

"Fine," Bryan said and walked away. "If you don't want to tell me, then there isn't anything I can do to help you. Have it your way."

Sarah looked after her brother as he left the living room, feeling awful for keeping this from him. If only he knew what she risked, then he would understand. Sarah sighed, then got up, walked to her bedroom, and closed the door behind her. She sat with her back against it for a few hours, catching her breath, listening to all the sounds, jumping every time a car drove up the street outside, wondering if this could be the one—if this were the red pick-up truck coming for her.

Chapter 57

"You've got to be kidding me."

I stared at Scott as Chief Annie brought him out to me. He slumped his head and got into my minivan. His own car had been taken to the impound again after he was arrested, and he wouldn't be able to get it until the next day, they said.

"Make sure he is taken out of my town and doesn't come back here," Annie said.

I nodded and got in. I started the engine with an angry movement, and it roared to life.

"I'm sorry, Eva Rae," he said. "For having to ask for your help again. You're the only one I knew would come and get me."

"Because I am just that stupid," I said and stepped on the accelerator, driving the minivan out of the parking lot behind the police station. It was late and very dark outside now. Chief Annie was the one who called me and told me to come to get Scott once they were done with him.

"No, that's not what I meant. Not at all," he said. "Please, don't say that."

"Then what is it, Scott? Why am I suddenly so important in

184

your life? Why is it I constantly have to throw up everything I have in my hands and come tend to your many emergencies?"

He exhaled. "I'm sorry. What do you want me to say?"

"What were you even doing at her house? She said you had been stalking her. What is going on with you, Scott? Stalking young girls? What happened to you?"

He gave me a look, then focused his gaze on the window. We drove for about ten minutes without anyone saying anything, then as we went over the bridges towards Viera, where Scott lived, he looked at me again.

"Do you ever wonder what our lives would be like if we had chosen differently?"

I swallowed, feeling my stomach turn to knots. I had been thinking about exactly that a lot lately.

"What do you mean?"

He shook his head. "Nothing. I just wonder sometimes. There's a lot in my life I would have liked to do differently now, looking back."

"I think most people feel that way," I said. "Life is messy. But at the end of it, I do like to believe we look back at it and say that we made the most of what we had been dealt."

He nodded. "I sure hope so. I hate to think I wasted it."

I looked out the window while driving, wondering about him. I couldn't stop thinking about Sarah and the way she had looked at him when we faced her in Winter Park. It was strange. She really didn't want him. What had happened between them? Had Scott hurt her? Was that why he was stalking that girl too? Because he was some creep that hurt women?

If so, then why was I helping him again? Just because he had no one else? Or was I deeper in than I thought? After what happened in Winter Park, I had promised myself I never wanted to see him again, yet I came running as soon as Annie called.

Was he just a creep? Was Matt right, and I was completely blind?

I drove up in front of his townhouse and parked. He turned to look at me, then smiled.

"Listen, I know I haven't exactly shown myself from my best side lately. But I want to thank you for believing in me when no one else did. And for helping me out tonight, again."

"The girl is getting a restraining order on you, so you better stay clear of her from now on," I said. "And Chief Annie told you to stay out of her town, so you should probably listen to that too. If she catches you speeding, she'll take you back in, and this time, she won't be as merciful."

He scoffed. "Wow. I can't believe it has come to this. Unwanted in my old hometown. Well, if it can't be any different, then I guess so be it."

"That's the deal, Scott; you better honor it."

He grabbed the door handle and was about to leave when he paused. "I meant you and me. You know that, right?"

"What?"

"When I talked about regrets. I was talking about us. Don't you wonder what it would have been like if we had become a couple instead of just sneaking around? If we had stayed together?"

I stared at him, speechless. I had wondered that so many times lately, but I didn't want to. I didn't want to think about how deeply I had been in love with him, even though we just fooled around. I had wanted him so badly back then, wanted him to choose me over Hannah, and hoped he would break up with her because he realized his great love for me was more profound than what he had with her. But when it did happen, when she broke up with him, he didn't choose me after all. He didn't even call me or come looking for me. He just left town after graduation, and we never saw one another again. It was the biggest heartbreak of my life, and he didn't even know it. Now, he was seriously looking at me and telling me he regretted it too?

"Did you want to?" I asked, not sure I wanted to hear the answer.

"Heck, yeah," he said. "I was nuts about you. I used to come to see you run track all the time, just to see you."

"But you were with Hannah," I said. "You were homecoming queen and king. You were the perfect couple."

"I know," he said. "It was all an image thing. We felt we belonged together because we belonged to the same group. You know how things were back then. It didn't matter if you liked her or not. It was just how it was supposed to be, right? And then she broke up with me, and I was so excited, I could have burst."

I tilted my head. "Really? Why did she say you tried to run her over?"

He scoffed. "I told her I was relieved when she broke up with me, and I think she was just upset about that. She wanted me to be heartbroken. She knew I wasn't really into her and us. She could feel it, and I think she wanted to punish me. She made up this rumor that I had tried to hurt her because I didn't want her to leave me. I never touched her. All I could think about was the fact that I was now a free man and could date you."

I could barely breathe. Scott turned his head and faced me, pushing himself closer to me as he spoke. My heart throbbed in my chest, and I couldn't find the words. For so many years, I cried over this guy, and here he was telling me he wanted me back then. And maybe now too.

"But...but you never called or said anything after you and Hannah broke up," I said. "Why didn't you?"

His eyes grew confused. "What do you mean? I called your house. I spoke to your mom and told her to tell you to call me back. When you didn't, I called again the next day and continued for several weeks in a row. It was right after graduation. When you never returned any of my calls, I concluded that you didn't want me, and I went away for college in Jacksonville. I was heartbroken—completely destroyed."

"But...but...oh, dear Lord. My mom must have deliberately not given me those messages because she didn't like you," I said, clutching the steering wheel hard between my fingers. "It sounds like something she would do. I can't believe it. I thought you didn't want me. I thought I was nothing but casual sex to you. I thought you just used me because Hannah wouldn't sleep with you."

Scott looked at me intently, then leaned toward me. He closed his eyes and placed a kiss on my lips. His lips were soft and tasted sweet, and I closed my eyes and kissed him back, tasting him. When our lips parted, he looked at me, looked deep into my eyes.

"I was nuts about you. You were so hot; I could've died. And to be honest, I still am crazy about you. Seeing you again has opened up all those old emotions. How could I not be? You were the one who got away. I came to you because I wanted help finding Sarah and getting my name cleared, and you did all that. But I had no idea what seeing you again would do to me."

With that, he winked and opened the door to the car. I watched him walk up to his townhouse, waving at me before he went inside, my heart throbbing so hard that it hurt my ribcage.

Chapter 58

T HEN:
     They were having a dinner party for some friends. Lynn and her boyfriend Stan looked at one another, and he put his arm around her shoulder while the woman from his office, Stella, talked about her and Phillip's trip to Europe a few weeks earlier. They had been on a Mediterranean cruise and traveled through Greece on a moped and seen Rome by car. It was fascinating to hear about, and when Stella walked to the bathroom, Stan leaned over and kissed Lynn's cheek, then whispered, "Next year, it's our turn. Let's go on a trip like that."

Lynn smiled and nodded, sipping her wine and feeling happy. She and Stan had been fighting a lot over the last couple of years. She had begun to wonder if they'd last—if their love for one another was even enough. But lately, they had been doing a lot better, and she was enjoying him again. She was beginning to think they might make it after all. She leaned over and kissed his cheek with a light laugh. As she pulled back, her phone's display lit up, and Stan noticed since it was lying on the table in front of them.

Stan looked at his watch. "It's almost ten o'clock at night. Who is calling you at this hour?"

She looked at the display. She didn't recognize the number and thought about letting it go to voicemail but then picked it up anyway.

"It's Jeff," the voice said on the other end. He sounded agitated, almost out of breath. Lynn jumped to her feet and hurried out of the room, hoping that no one could hear it was a male voice.

"What are you doing?" she asked angrily when she was in the hallway. "You can't call me!"

"But…but I miss you so much," he said. "I don't know what you've done to me, but I can't function properly. I can only think about you. All the time, Doc, do you hear me? It's *all* the time."

She sighed and leaned her head against the wall behind her. She had let him go too far, and she knew it. This wasn't good at all.

"Jeff, you can't call me."

"Why not? I just wanted to hear your voice."

"It's not good, Jeff. Besides, I am in a relationship. You know this. If he finds out you're calling me, he'll leave me."

Jeff went quiet. "Okay. I'm sorry."

She sighed and closed her eyes. "Are you okay, Jeff?"

"I don't know," he said. "You tell me."

"What do you mean?"

A long pause followed.

"Turn around."

Lynn opened her eyes and did as he said. Then, she froze. There he was, standing right outside the window, looking in. Seeing his longing eyes made her heart melt completely, and she hung up, then stared at him through the glass for a few seconds before moving toward the door leading to the porch. She walked outside, closed the door behind her, and they stood in the rain, staring deeply into one another's eyes.

Then, he leaned over, grabbed her face between his hands, and kissed her. She kissed him back, and he lifted her up. He placed her on the patio furniture table, then pressed himself up against her while pulling up her skirt.

Chapter 59

I didn't sleep at all that night. Frustratingly enough, it wasn't because of the babies. For once, they actually slept through the night, both of them and I could have had the chance to catch up on some much-needed sleep. But I didn't. All I could think about was Scott and that kiss we shared. I listened to Matt's heavy breathing in bed next to me, feeling the guilt nag at me in my stomach.

What am I doing? What is happening to me?

Needless to say, I felt awful, and it continued the next morning. For some reason—probably guilt—I was being extra nice to Matt and made him his favorite breakfast with scrambled eggs and freshly baked chocolate chip muffins. The kids ate as if I had never fed them before, then left for school. Matt stayed behind, drinking his coffee, sitting at the breakfast counter, while scrolling through Facebook. My father, grandmother, and brother were there too, chatting along, but Matt didn't really talk to them. I got the feeling he was getting pretty annoyed with them being here. I couldn't blame him. It was a lot.

"How about you and I go out for dinner tonight, huh?" I asked, leaning over the counter. "My dad and grandmother can watch the babies."

He didn't look up from his phone but sipped his coffee. "What's that?"

"Matt, look at me."

He lifted his gaze and met mine. I felt like throwing up; that's how much the guilt was eating at me.

"I asked if you wanted to go out to dinner tonight. We could go to Pompano Grill? You love that place. It'll be just the two of us. It's my family's last night here, and we need to take advantage of having all these potential babysitters in the house."

He gave me half a smile. "Sure. Whatever you want. You're the boss around here anyway, right?"

He drank the rest of his coffee, grabbed his keys, and left. I stared at the door as it slammed shut, then exhaled.

"Are you two all right?" My dad asked.

I shook my head, trying not to look as sad as I felt inside. "Going through a rough patch. But I hope we will be."

I called Pompano Grill and reserved a table, then texted Matt to be there at six-thirty and added a heart emoji. I fed the babies, then put them down for their nap when my phone vibrated. Thinking—and hoping—it was Matt who called to say how much he still loved me, I pulled it out of my pocket in a swift motion, only to realize I didn't recognize the number. I picked it up anyway.

"Bryan Abbey here."

I paused. It was Sarah's brother. Why was he calling me?

"Bryan? What can I do for you?"

"It's my sister," he said.

"She's back...or so I've heard," I said, trying not to reveal the fact that we went to his house.

"Yes, she came back, but she wasn't quite herself. She kept sitting at the window, gun in her hand, guarding the house like she was expecting someone to come after her."

"Did she say anything about where she had been or what happened to her?" I asked.

"Only that she had been taken and held against her will. She wouldn't reveal where she had been or if she knew who had kidnapped her. I got the feeling she did, though. I begged her to go to the police, but she wouldn't do that either."

"That's odd. Do you think she was protecting this person, whoever it was?"

He sighed. "I don't know. She seemed scared to talk to the police somehow. She was scared of everything. And now, well, I was about to leave for work, but she hadn't come out of her room. So, I went in to say goodbye, but she wasn't there. Her bed was empty. I searched the house and the yard outside, but she's not here."

I sat down in the rocking chair behind me, where I usually sat with the babies when they woke up at night, trying to get them back to sleep. I cupped my mouth.

"She has disappeared again?"

"It would appear so, yes. Please, help me find her. I'm worried something bad has happened to her again. What if that person came back for her?"

I nodded, understanding his worry. "Was there any sign of forced entry?"

"Not that I can see, no. But the back door was left unlocked. I don't know if she left that way or if we forgot to lock it, and this person came in through there and took her again. Please, help me find her, will you? I don't have a good feeling about this."

Chapter 60

I left the babies safely—at least I hoped so—in the hands of my family, my grandmother and dad, then told them I would only be gone for a few hours. I left, guilt nagging once again in the pit of my stomach, and drove toward Winter Park. I didn't say anything to Matt about me leaving. I didn't want him to tell me that I could just say no when he knew perfectly well that wasn't an option for me. I had gotten myself involved in this strange story and couldn't just let it go now. I knew he wouldn't understand. Besides, he didn't have to know. He was gone all day, and I would be back before he was off from work. I stopped at a Seven-Eleven to get myself some coffee and a soda, then continued toward Orlando while wondering—and worrying deeply—about this news.

Sarah had disappeared again. Was this woman just a master of vanishing dramatically, or had something happened to her? She had told her brother she was kidnapped and held against her will. If that was true, then had this person come for her again? Was this person determined to finish her off?

Or was something else entirely going on?

I needed to know. I needed to get to the bottom of this story before I could let it go. I would keep digging until my fingers bled before giving up. It would end up haunting me if I hadn't done everything in my power to help her.

I just wished Matt would understand that about me.

I speculated if I should tell Scott about Bryan's call, but something made me not call him. Was it because of the kiss we had shared? Or was it that I feared he had played me all along and maybe come back to hurt Sarah? He had surprised me many times over, and I had to admit, I found it hard to trust him. He had never offered me any explanation as to why he was stalking that girl, Lily. It was creepy to me, and along with the other stuff that had been revealed about him lately, I could no longer deny that I felt like I had to be careful with him. I mean, he seemed to have an explanation for everything. Hannah had made it up, Sarah had fallen by accident, and Lily had misunderstood his intentions on the bridge. But that didn't explain why he kept stalking her? Why didn't he try to explain that to me?

And then, of course, there was the kiss we had shared. I guess I didn't really want to face him after that.

I parked in front of the old home on Howell Branch Road, then walked through the long front yard, up to the porch. Some of the grass and leaves had turned brown due to the lack of rain. It had been an unusually dry winter this year. Yet the yard still looked impeccable.

Bryan opened the door when I knocked. He seemed out of breath, agitated, and he was sweating heavily.

"Can I come in?"

He let me, and I walked inside.

"Did she sleep in here?"

He nodded, and I walked into the bedroom. The bed was made, and it didn't look like it had been slept in at all. She could have been gone already last night for all we knew. It would be no use to go out searching for her. She could be far gone already.

"I left everything the way I found it this morning as you told me to," he said.

"This is all?"

"She doesn't have much stuff. She didn't bring anything with her when she came back. She threw out the clothes she was wearing. They were completely destroyed. I had never seen anything like it. She was in a terrible state when she came here but assured me she didn't need to go to the hospital. I did notice some bruises on her wrists and her arms, though, but she wouldn't tell me how she got them. I bought her some pants and shirts at Walmart that she could wear. She didn't want to leave the house, she said. She just sat in that chair by the window like she was waiting for someone to come get her. It was really eerie, to be honest. But she wouldn't tell me who it was, who had hurt her, who she was waiting for. I could just see that she was scared."

"It's much like what she did in Viera," I said while scanning the room, looking for anything that could tell me what had happened to her, if she had left willingly or not. I was mostly looking for signs of a struggle—a tipped-over lamp or trace of blood on the floor.

"What do you mean?"

"Nothing. It's just that…she was dating Scott when she disappeared. And she said to him a couple of months ago that if she ever went missing, he should go looking for her. It just tells me she knew someone was searching for her. She was afraid of someone. That's why I would really like to know what—or who—she ran from when leaving Winter Park three years ago."

I walked around to the other side of the bed, my eyes scanning everything I could see but found nothing—no signs of a struggle. That didn't mean she hadn't been taken against her will. A gun to the head or a knife to the throat was enough to make people come along quietly. I glanced toward the chair by the window and tried to picture her sitting there, then remembered seeing her come out to us when we were last there.

Gun clutched in her hand.

"She had a gun," I said.

"Yes, she was using my gun; it made her feel protected," Bryan said, then wrinkled his forehead. "How did you know that?"

"I was just guessing," I lied, not wanting to explain how I knew and get into the discussion of why Sarah would put a gun to Scott's head if they were dating. It still had me greatly puzzled, and I kept wondering what the heck he did to her. "But where is that gun now?"

Bryan looked confused. "Let me check if she put it back."

He left and came back a few minutes later. "It's not in the box under my bed where it usually is."

"So, technically, she could still have it?" I asked.

"I...I guess so."

I nodded. "You and I are going to make some coffee, and then we'll sit down and have a long chat. I need you to tell me everything, and I mean everything about Sarah. When she lived here, who did she hang out with? Where did she work? Where did she live? Who were her coworkers? What school did she attend? Did she have any enemies? Any heart she broke? Any big events in her life? Anything that might have happened back then that could justify her leaving everyone just like that. You must have had an idea back then about what could make her suddenly pick up and leave. I need to know everything. Do you hear me, Bryan? Everything. Don't leave out a single thing."

Chapter 61

THEN:

"They're here again. The detectives are here."

Lynn stared at her secretary, who bore a nervous smile.

"They're in the waiting room."

Lynn nodded. "Give me a minute to get myself ready, then send them in."

Lynn rushed to her office and put down her briefcase, heart bouncing in her chest. Why were they here? Did they know about her and Jeff? What they had done was dangerous, especially for her. Having sex with a client was a third-degree felony, and she risked losing her license and maybe even jail time. Was that why they were here?

"Can we come in?" Detective Fraser said as he peeked in the door.

Lynn composed herself and straightened her shirt. She tried to smile, even though she knew it would come off as awkward.

"Of course, come on in."

It was the same two as the last time they had been there—Detective Fraser and Detective Harder. The first one had grown a beard since the last time she saw him. It made him look sloppy.

Lynn had never liked men with beards. She preferred them clean-shaven.

Like Jeff.

"What can I do for you today, Detectives?" she asked when they sat down. She felt how shaky her hands were and placed them in her lap so they wouldn't see.

Detective Fraser cleared his throat. "We're here about Jeffrey Johnson, your patient. Again."

She tilted her head. "You know I can't discuss my patients."

"Yes, yes, we do know. But the thing is…" Fraser looked at Harder before continuing. "Well, the thing is…that it is now officially a murder case."

Lynn stopped breathing. "A…a murder case?"

Harder nodded, then took over. "We found Joanna Harry's body in a lake behind Jeffrey Johnson's house."

"We believe your client, Jeff Johnson, had kept her locked up somewhere, then later killed her. She was kept in a place with little to no sunlight and was terribly malnourished before her death, the autopsy showed."

Lynn stared at them, barely able to breathe.

"Excuse me?"

"We think she might have been kept in a basement or something like it for quite some time. And then he decided to kill her."

"I…I'm not sure I understand."

"Her body was bruised, especially on the wrists, telling us she was kept in chains. She was found with blunt force trauma to the back of her head. She suffered several fractures to the skull, and we believe that is the cause of her death."

"And you think my client…did all this to her?"

Fraser nodded. "Yes. He's officially our main suspect, and we want to talk to him."

"But he's disappeared," Harder said. "We haven't been able to locate him. We went to his house with a warrant and didn't find him or the basement."

"But that doesn't mean he didn't do it," Fraser said. "He might have had another place he kept her, and we were wondering if he ever spoke of another place, a summer house, a cabin in the mountains up north, or maybe a beach shack? Did he go anywhere to unwind?"

Lynn barely blinked. "I...not that I recall right now, but I will go through his file and all my notes and look, of course."

They stood. Fraser handed her a card. "And then, we'd, of course, ask you to let us know if he shows his face here again. If he shows up to his next appointment, then please call this number. Keep him here until we can get here."

Lynn nodded nervously while images of them on her patio table rushed through her mind—his hands on her breasts, his lips on her neck. She could still hear his heavy breathing in her ear, and it made her shiver.

"N-naturally, of course."

Chapter 62

"I can't really think of what exactly could have made her leave," Bryan said and leaned back on the couch in his living room. We had been through all her childhood, her school friends, then later her co-workers from the hardware store where she worked, and all her close friends. Nothing seemed to stand out, and now the coffee pot was empty.

I leaned forward, rubbing my forehead while looking at my notes. "Wasn't there anything that would give her a reason to want to disappear—anything at all? Did something happen to her? Her boyfriend Tommy died, but that wasn't until after she had left, right?"

"It was six months after, actually."

"I just have this feeling that it is somehow related to him," I said, knowing we had been down this path before. "What's happening now—I just can't seem to connect the dots."

Bryan's gaze became distant, and he turned his head away. "There were days when I wondered if she had killed him. If she had come back to do it, or maybe stayed close by all the time."

"Would Sarah be capable of something like that?" I asked.

He shook his head. "Not the Sarah I knew, but..."

"But what?"

"She wasn't completely herself before she disappeared. I got the feeling she wasn't well."

"And why do you think you had that feeling?"

He shrugged, then lowered his head. "No reason. It's just a feeling; that's all. She was different somehow."

"How so?"

"She became introverted, pulled back and into herself. She wouldn't talk to me or Tommy about it. Tommy came to me and said he was worried too."

"Okay, okay, this is good," I said. "Why didn't you mention this earlier?"

He looked at me. "As I said, it was just a feeling. I wasn't even sure it was important, or if I just imagined things."

"Was there anything else different about her?" I asked.

"She seemed angrier. She got upset easier, and she spent a lot of time on her phone, texting. Tommy feared she was seeing someone else, but that isn't like my sister. She's very loyal. Our dad cheated on our mom, and she hated him for it. But Tommy did say they never had sex anymore, that she didn't want to. He also said she was often awake at night, unable to sleep."

"She had a lot on her mind, maybe," I said.

I wondered for a minute if she had already met Scott at this point and just didn't know how to tell Tommy. Had Scott then persuaded her to leave everyone behind and then killed Tommy? He could be very charming and charismatic when he wanted to. I had felt how persuasive he was on myself lately. And then, when Sarah wanted to leave Scott, he locked her up and made up the story of her disappearing because he thought it would be believable since she had done so before? He alerted the police, filled out a missing person's report. Then he came to me to make sure it seemed legit? He engaged me in finding her so it would seem like he was truly looking for her and help him get the police off his back? But then, things didn't entirely go as planned. Sarah escaped somehow, and he didn't know where she was? Was that why I didn't hear from him for quite some time? Because he was looking for her? And then, I helped him find her again? Had I helped him do that? The thought was devastating. But it would explain why she stuck the gun in our faces.

"Did she know this guy?" I asked. I found a picture I had kept from my research online. It was taken from his Instagram account. "His name is Jeffrey Johnson."

Bryan looked at it, then shook his head. "I don't think so. I've never seen him before."

I put the phone back. "Okay. And you have no idea if she was seeing someone else then, or who it was?"

Bryan shook his head. "I just don't get it, though. She would never betray Tommy. It simply wasn't her."

Chapter 63

She snuck around the house and found the back door. She grabbed the handle and pulled it, but it was locked. Gun clutched in hand, Sarah turned to the window next to the door and realized it was unlocked. She pulled it open, then slid inside on the floor, landing with a thud, making too much noise for her liking.

She hurried to her feet, then rushed to the kitchen, where she found her target sitting in a chair, back turned to her. Holding her breath, tiptoeing closer, sweat springing to her forehead, Sarah crept closer until she could almost smell this person. She placed the gun on their neck.

"Took you long enough," the voice said.

The person spun their head like an owl and looked directly at her. Hands shaking, Sarah placed the gun on the person's forehead and cocked it.

"Don't you dare move. I will shoot."

A smile spread across the target's face. Sarah shivered when seeing it. So many times, she had looked at that smile while in the hole.

"No, you won't, Sarah." A hand was reached out toward her and caressed her cheek gently. The hand was placed on her neck, and her head pulled closer, so she could smell the breath of the person speaking. "You want to know why you won't?"

Their eyes locked, and Sarah felt herself soften. She exhaled and bit her lip. Then she shook her head, pulling back.

"I don't want you to speak at all."

The person sighed. "You won't kill me, Sarah, because you love me. Do you remember that? Do you recall how much you love me?"

Sarah felt her heart rate go up as she pressed the gun against the person's forehead. "I will kill you if I have to."

That made the person smile.

"Really?"

"Really. I don't love you anymore."

"Is that what you've been telling yourself? You don't know yourself very well, Sarah. I do. I knew you'd come back. That's how well I know you."

"You don't know me at all."

A patronizing head tilt made Sarah almost lose it in anger. She pressed the gun hard into the skin and panted as she considered pulling the trigger.

"I would have done anything for you," the voice said. "But you hurt me."

"I hate you," Sarah said, spitting the words. "I hate you so much!"

"Tsk, tsk, Sarah. Just put the gun down, and let's have a real talk. I know you're angry that I trapped you in the basement, but what did you want me to do? You were going to run away again. I couldn't let you run. You need to learn how to face your demons. You can't run every time anything gets tough."

Sarah stared at the face in front of her, nostrils flaring. She wanted so badly to pull the trigger, to finish it here and now—end of story.

But could she?

Another smile spread across the person's face. "See? I told you so."

The person placed a hand on her arm, and she felt herself melt. Her feelings for this person were still so deep, so profound, even after all that had happened. It was like a spell. The softness in the other person's eyes got to her, made her a prisoner, almost paralyzed her.

She lowered the gun.

I should never have come back. I should have known this would happen.

"There you go," the person said, still looking into her eyes, stripping her of all will and strength. "Put the gun down, and then we'll talk. Come. Give it to me. There you go."

Sarah was about to hand over the gun when she hesitated.

It'll never stop. If you don't fight it now, then you'll never be able to free yourself.

"That's it; hand me the gun. Sarah?"

Sarah shook her head and took a step back, tears springing to her eyes.

"No," she said and lifted the gun again. "I can't do this anymore. It has to end now."

Tears welling up in her eyes, making it hard to see properly, she pulled the trigger.

Chapter 64

The sun was beginning to set behind the tall trees on Bryan's property. I watched it from the window at his house, a worrying sensation nagging in the pit of my stomach. Sarah was in trouble, whether or not she had left this house willingly. I had to find her somehow. I simply had to.

Before it was too late.

I called my dad back home and asked how the babies were doing. I felt so guilty for leaving them this long.

"They're great," he answered, much to my relief. I had been worried for no reason. "We're having a blast with them."

"Really?"

"Sure. Right now, they're down for another nap, so that gives us time to cook dinner for tonight, or rather your grandmother is doing that. Adam and I are just hanging out. I'm doing some work. Olivia and Christine are helping granny in the kitchen while Alex is watching TV with us. Elijah is in his room, probably playing computer games. All the kids are alive and breathing, so that's good, right?"

Good? It sounded like he was way better at taking care of my family than I was. I exhaled, suddenly feeling exhausted.

"You sound troubled," he said. "Still no news about Sarah Abbey?"

I pinched the bridge of my nose and closed my eyes briefly. "No. I'm concerned about her."

I wanted to tell him that I worried Scott had played me, but I didn't want him to know what a fool I had been for trusting him. I had let myself be blinded by my infatuation and not listened to the alarm signals going off in my head.

"Where does the trace end?"

"We were talking about her boyfriend, the one who was killed. And that's where we got stuck. If only I knew if it really was Jeffrey Johnson's truck that hit him. But it was destroyed in the fire."

My dad went quiet for a few seconds. "Let me check something."

I could hear him tapping on the keyboard. "Yup. Just as I suspected."

"What?"

"According to the fire investigation report, there was no car in the garage at the time of the fire."

"Excuse me?"

"It could still be out there somewhere."

"But...but his sister said it had been destroyed in the fire," I said, rubbing my forehead.

My dad became silent again.

"Sister? What sister? I researched this guy for you, and no sister was mentioned anywhere. No, I just checked again. It says here he was an only child."

My eyes grew wide, and I clenched the phone against my skin while a million thoughts rushed through my mind. I hung up without saying goodbye, then looked at Bryan, sitting next to me.

"Can I borrow your computer for a second?" I asked. "There's something I need to check."

Chapter 65

T HEN:
    "Jeff is here."

The secretary was as pale as the wall behind her when she peeked inside Lynn's office. "Do you want me to call the police?"

Lynn stared at her, holding her breath. He was here? He had come? She had genuinely believed he wouldn't show up for his appointment while being on the run from the police and all that. Why had he come?

He might tell on you. He might tell the police you two had sex, and then you'll go down with him.

Lynn barely blinked, then said, "Not yet. Wait for my signal. Let him in."

"O-okay."

Pretend like you don't know. When he steps in, make sure he doesn't suspect you have been talking to the police.

"Doc!"

Lynn looked up from her notepad, then smiled. "Jeffrey. How wonderful to see you. How are you today? Take your time to answer."

Slow down. You're speaking too fast. He'll notice.

He sat down with a deep exhale. His hair was tousled, and he hadn't shaved. "A lot has happened, Doc. You won't believe it."

Lynn nodded. "Try me."

He exhaled again, got himself comfortable on the couch, then lifted his gaze and met hers. "They…they think I killed Joanna. They found her body in the lake, and…they're after me, Doc. I don't know what to do. I've been staying at a friend's house, but they'll come for me there too. I just know they will."

Lynn nodded, trying to act surprised. "Now, I want you to calm down, Jeff. Take a few deep breaths and make sure you're feeling calm, okay? Let's talk about this."

Jeff leaned back. His nostrils were flaring, but he seemed calmer. "I knew you'd understand, Doc. I knew you'd listen to me. No one else will."

She nodded. "Absolutely."

"The thing is, Doc, I don't know how to get out of this. I've tried to tell them I didn't touch her, that I never would."

Lynn looked at him, eyes narrowing. "But you did say to me that you sometimes fantasized about locking her up in your basement. Do you remember that?"

He paused. He sat there, staring at her. Had she gone too far?

"Do you remember saying that to me?" she asked.

"Well…yes…but…could you stop writing for a second there, Doc?"

Lynn stopped and looked up from her pad again.

"Okay."

"Do you write everything I say down?" he then asked. "I mean that thing about the basement; it would look really bad if the police got ahold of that."

Lynn stared at him, not answering. "I see."

"What have you been writing on that pad, Doc?" he asked, his eyes lingering on Lynn's hand holding the pen. "Can I see it?"

Lynn shook her head. "No, Jeff, you can't."

Before she could react, he stood to his feet, walked to her, and pulled the notepad out from between her hands. She tried to grab it back from him, but he was too fast, and soon his eyes were scanning the paper. Then he looked at her, a deep furrow growing between his eyes.

"What's this? Why haven't you written anything I said on the notepad?" he turned the pad to show her. "All it says here is *I killed her. I killed Joanna?*" He stared at her, mouth gaping.

"What's that supposed to mean?"

Chapter 66

The gun went off, and the blast pushed Sarah back. Meanwhile, her target ducked down, jumped for her, and grabbed around her legs, making her fall. Her back hit the tiles below with a thud. The bullet had missed and hit the cabinet at the other end of the kitchen.

She had missed.

The person was soon on top of her, punching her face and knocking the gun out of her hand, so it slid across the tiles. More punches followed and excruciating pain, and soon Sarah saw nothing but stars in a sea of blackness.

She could taste her own blood as she was being dragged by the hair across the tiles, turned around, and tied up using duct tape. She lay there, fighting to remain conscious while the person stood above her, panting, gun in hand.

"You never should have come back, Sarah. It wasn't a very smart move. But then again, you never were that clever, were you?"

Sarah groaned behind the duct tape that was covering her lips. She really did feel stupid right now. If only she had kept running instead of staying with her brother. If only she had gotten out of here while there was still time.

You're stupid, Sarah. You really are stupid!

The question now was what would happen to her next. Would she end up back in the chains in the room in the basement? Would she be kept down there for what felt like another eternity? Living off the mercy of her capturer? Or would she be killed right there on the kitchen floor?

Sarah cried and whimpered as the person bent down, placed a kiss on her forehead, and then looked into her eyes.

"I'm sorry it had to end this way, Sarah. I really am. But it's over now. We're over. No need to drag it out. Let's end this now."

The person walked away for a few minutes and then returned with a big sledgehammer between their hands.

"A gun makes too much noise."

Sarah stared at the huge sledgehammer, heart dropping. She wanted to beg and plead for her life, but she knew it would be no use. She was going to die a violent and gruesome death right here on this kitchen floor.

It really was over.

Sarah closed her eyes and laid her head down on the cold tile, waiting for the pain, hoping and praying it would be over quickly, that it wouldn't take more than one blow for her to die.

She waited for it, coming to terms with the fact that it was all over, while the person lifted the sledgehammer and let it whistle through the air when suddenly a noise coming from outside the house made everything stop, the hammer dangling mid-air.

It was the sound of a car door slamming shut.

Sarah lifted her head, tears streaming across her cheeks, then looked toward the door where footsteps were approaching, and soon the doorbell rang. She could barely breathe behind the tape, and as her heart throbbed in her chest, her mind suddenly overwhelmed with hope.

Someone's at the front door! Someone is here!

Chapter 67

It was pitch dark out as I walked up toward the old two-story house. In daylight, it had looked so pretty with its white wood, green-shuttered windows, and an old-Florida style entrance that was sheltered from the often-heavy rain. Not to mention the lush yard that surrounded it and the lake in the background. But in the dark, it suddenly seemed beyond creepy. Maybe it was just the situation.

I took a deep breath, then rang the doorbell.

Nothing happened.

I rang it again, then knocked.

"Hello? Isabella Hayton? Hello?"

A few seconds went by, and then the door swung open. The tall, slender woman stood in front of me, wearing her suit jacket and black skirt. Her alabaster skin seemed paler than the last time I had seen her.

"Yes? Oh, it's you again. What do you want?"

I was about to speak when she interrupted me.

"Listen, I have had a really long day. I've told you everything I know about my brother and the fire. I don't have the…"

I pulled out my badge and showed it to her. "I'm looking for Sarah Abbey. I have reason to believe she might be here."

Isabella stared at my badge, then up at my face. She lifted her nose toward the sky and looked down at me, her lower lip lightly vibrating as she spoke again, "Well, she's not. There's no one here. Now, if you'll excuse me, I…"

She was about to close the door when I put a foot in to block it.

"Not so fast."

Isabella stared at my foot, then up at me. "Excuse me?"

"I have a question that has been bothering me," I said.

"Oh, by all means, do tell," she said. "I am *dying* to know what it is."

I sent her a sarcastic smile. "Could you please explain to me why you told me your name is Isabella Hayton when the name of the person who owns and lives in the house is something else, according to the official records?"

Isabella narrowed her eyes. "My mother bought it for me. She still keeps her address here."

"Really?"

Isabella gave me a look. She was a good liar but obviously unaware that her lower lip quivered when she did.

"Yes, really. Now, I need to go…"

"What if I tell you I don't think you're Jeffrey Johnson's sister at all?"

"Excuse me?"

The vibration became worse, and she knew she was revealed. The question was what she'd do next. I kept my right hand on the handle of my gun in the holster on my back.

"What if I tell you he didn't have a sister?"

Her lips grew tight. She shook her head.

"That's just…"

"A lie? Reality? Do you even know the difference anymore?"

"I am not going to stand here and listen to this…" she trailed off.

"You were his therapist, weren't you? It says so in the police report. It says that the detectives went to you to find him when he ran from the police in connection with the murder of his ex-girlfriend, Joanna Harry. They went to talk to his therapist, Lynn

Parks, which is, funnily enough, the name of the owner of this house."

The woman in front of me was barely moving.

"Did you buy this house to be closer to him? It says in the official papers that you bought it a year before he died in that fire. Why did you do that? You were obsessed with him, weren't you? This way, you could keep an eye on him constantly. You could make sure he didn't see other women. It's not unusual to have sexual feelings for your patients or vice versa. It's actually very normal in a therapeutic setting, but you took it too far, didn't you? And it spiraled out of control for you."

Chapter 68

T HEN:
   "What the heck is this supposed to mean? Doc?"
Jeff held the notepad tightly between his hands, then turned it and showed it to Lynn. His eyes were torn in disbelief.

"*I...killed her?*" Jeff continued, then flipped a page, then another. "Why have you written that all over your notepad? Hundreds of times on each and every page?"

Lynn tried to smile. "Jeff. Sit down, and then we can talk. You're agitated. Please, calm yourself down."

A deep furrow had grown between his eyes, and it wasn't easing up. "Is it true? Did...did you kill Joanna?"

Lynn exhaled. "Absolutely."

"W-what?"

She lifted her hand. "I did it for you, Jeff."

He shook his head, then paced back and forth. "You did it for me? What's that even supposed to mean? I don't understand anything right now...I...can't breathe...please, tell me this is some sick joke."

She closed her eyes briefly. His agitation annoyed her. Nothing good ever came from being frantic—only rash, stupid decisions.

"Jeff," she said, using her authoritative voice, looking up at him. "She hurt you. She hurt you so deeply when she left you."

He looked appalled. "So...you...kidnapped her and kept her in your...basement?"

Lynn smiled secretively. "Well, you gave me the idea for that one. I thought it was fitting. I invited her over to my new house, telling her I needed to talk to her about you, and then I slipped a sedative into her iced tea. I kept her down there for a couple of months. We got into a fight one day when she was trying to escape, and she fell and hurt the back of her head. I took her body to the lake by our houses and dumped her, thinking the alligators would get rid of the body, but well...you know the rest."

Jeff stared down at her, not blinking. His lips were parted like he wanted to speak but couldn't find the words.

"So...you...you did all that to her? To Joanna? And now the police are searching for me?"

"Yes, that is most unfortunate."

Jeff ran a hand through his hair, then pulled on the sides of it. He finally sat down and hid his face between the hands.

"I'm gonna go to jail for this, for what you did?"

Lynn leaned forward and placed a hand on his knee. He looked up, and their eyes met. For a second, they shared a loving gaze; at least she believed they did, but then Jeff's went dark as a shadow came over his face.

"I'm gonna have to tell them about us. I'm going to have to tell them everything. About the kisses, about the sex, and about you... and what you've done."

Lynn's eyes grew wide for a second, and she pulled her hand back from his knee with a swift movement.

"You can't do that."

He rose to his feet. "But I have to. It's the only way. I'll tell them everything. Come clean."

Lynn shook her head.

"It's either that, or you will tell them everything, Doc. As you said, it was an accident. You didn't mean for her to die. I'll give you until the morning. If you haven't spoken to the police by then, I will."

Lynn opened her mouth to speak, but as she did, Jeff rose to his feet. He left before she could protest, slamming the door.

"Should I call the police now?" her secretary asked when he was gone.

Lynn composed herself, clenching her fists hard. Then she shook her head while controlling her breathing.

"No. Not yet. Let's give him some time to come to his senses."

Chapter 69

S arah heard the voices in the distance. They were getting louder and sounded like they were arguing now. She thought she had heard her own name mentioned, and that had filled her with a last ray of hope.

Had this person come looking for her?

I gotta make some noise somehow, let them know I'm here! It's my last and only chance.

Sarah tried to scream behind the duct tape, but not much sound left her mouth, not enough to reach them out by the front door from the kitchen floor where she was still lying. Lynn had put the sledge-hammer down by the end of the counter, and Sarah saw it now, then wondered if she could get close enough, if she could tip it over, and maybe somehow make a loud enough noise to let them know she was in there. Or perhaps she could get on her knees and pull something down from the counter?

Sarah tried to get up on her knees and spotted a plate not far away. If only she could get herself close enough.

Sarah laid back down on the cold tiles, then wormed her way across the floor. Then she rose to her knees again but slipped, and fell back down, face flat into the tiles. She whimpered in pain behind the duct tape as her head started to pound.

Sarah closed her eyes and cried before managing to press herself back up and onto her knees. It wasn't easy with her hands tied behind her back. She had to press her back up against the cabinet doors in order not to fall again and then slowly push herself upward. As she turned her head, she spotted the plate. It was right in front of her face, but she had no way of reaching it. She strained herself to try and pull her hands free but with no luck. And she couldn't get her face close enough to push it.

So close.

Sarah let herself slide back down, crying, and sat on the floor, while she could hear the voices grow more and more agitated by the door.

You have to let them know you're here. You have to! Come on, Sarah. Think of something. Think!

Sarah sighed and scanned the area around her. She was so exhausted, and hope was leaving her fast.

"You were his therapist, weren't you?" she heard a voice say.

Sarah's eyes shot open. This person wasn't only looking for her; she had actually figured Lynn out. She knew!

I'm here! I'm in here!

Sarah strained herself to worm a few inches further. She squirmed and squiggled until she could slide past the counter and now see the front door at the end of the living room. She could even see the woman's face, the one standing in the doorway talking to Lynn. She recognized her from the day she had come with Scott to her brother's house.

Help!

Sarah wiggled across the floor again when she spotted a big antique vase as tall as a small child with flowers in it by the corner. All she needed to do was to make it a little further, and then…

Sarah fought with all she had when she heard Lynn's voice say, "Now, I have had enough. I know my rights. If you don't have a warrant, then I will have to ask you to leave my property."

Hurry, Sarah, hurry!

Sarah pushed herself across the tiles and got closer and closer to the big vase, then turned around, so she could try and reach it with her legs when she heard the front door slam shut, and one second later, Lynn was standing above her, looking down at her, smiling.

"And what exactly do you think you're doing, huh?"

Sarah closed her eyes, then lifted both her tied-up legs into the air before slamming them into the vase.

Chapter 70

"I'm on my way home now."

I pressed the phone against my ear as I unlocked the minivan and was about to get in when I heard the loud crash coming from inside the house I had just left. My eyes grew wide, and I turned to stare at the front door that Lynn Parks had just slammed in my face, telling me she wasn't talking to me anymore unless I brought her a warrant.

"What was that?" I asked.

My dad grunted on the other end. "What was what?"

I kept looking at the house in front of me, my heart beating fast in my chest. My instinct told me I couldn't leave—not until I checked out what had made that loud noise.

"Never mind. I'm not coming home just yet," I said and hung up. I put the phone away, then grabbed my gun and pulled it out. I walked closer to a window, then hid next to it before peeking inside.

And right there, in the middle of the floor, I spotted Sarah Abbey. Her arms and legs were tied up, and Lynn Parks was hovering above her, slapping her face. The floor was covered in broken ceramic pieces, and flowers were spread onto the tiles. Lynn soon stopped, then pulled away. She disappeared, and a second later, she came back with a big sledgehammer between her hands.

I stared at her carrying that thing toward Sarah, and my heart completely stopped.

Then, I acted fast. I grabbed a garden gnome standing beneath the window, then threw it through the window, shattering it. The noise made Lynn turn her head and look toward me. I pointed my gun at her.

"Stop right there, Lynn!"

I used the gun to remove pieces of glass, so I could crawl through the window without cutting myself.

"Drop your weapon," I yelled at Lynn. "Drop the hammer, now!"

Lynn stared at me, hammer still held up in the air, then looked down at Sarah on the floor in visible distress, fear painted on her face.

"I'm serious, Lynn. I will shoot you if you don't drop the hammer now."

Lynn didn't even look at me. She just stood there like she was contemplating what would be worse—being shot or missing the opportunity to kill Sarah.

Finally, she decided to do as I said. She put it down on the floor, then looked at me, panting agitatedly. I approached her, my heart throbbing in my chest, gun pointed at her.

"Step away from the hammer," I said. "And from Sarah."

Lynn did as I told her and took one step back, then two. I knelt next to Sarah, still keeping my eyes fixated on Lynn, then removed the duct tape from her hands, legs, and mouth. Sarah cried and sat up, then hugged me, sobbing uncontrollably.

"She…she tried to kill me…she kept me in that basement… down there…"

Sarah pointed toward the stairs, and I nodded, then caressed her hair with the hand not holding the gun.

"I know. I know everything. The only thing I'm not quite sure of yet is how you two know one another and why she wanted to kill you."

Chapter 71

T HEN:

  Lynn was whistling while doodling on her notepad. She looked at her drawing—a house on fire, a man inside, lying in his bed, slowly perishing while flames were licking his body. What the beholder of the drawing couldn't possibly know—only Lynn did— was that the man was passed out. A sedative was slipped into his drink earlier that night, and then he was placed in bed with a lit cigarette between his fingers. Later, the forensics report would state that the fire originated in the bedroom from the cigarette that prob- ably caught the pillow on fire while the man was asleep. The toxi- cology report would later show he had taken sleeping pills. Suicide, some might conclude, but they'd never know for sure. But it made sense. He was, after all, suspected of having murdered his girlfriend. The police were onto him, and it all became too much for him. And his car? Lynn put it in her own garage before starting the fire. She needed it for later use. A vehicle that was believed ravaged in a fire could have all kinds of uses.

  "Your ten o'clock is here," her secretary said.

  Lynn tilted her head and studied her drawing to make sure she had gotten all the details in. Then she smiled and looked up at her secretary.

"I'm ready."

The secretary disappeared, and Lynn stared at her drawing, then ripped the page off and curled the paper up between her hands. She threw the ball of paper through the room, aiming for the trash bin in the corner. She hit it on her first shot just as her next patient came inside.

Lynn lifted her gaze and met that of the woman standing in the doorway. She was absolutely stunning, Lynn thought right away. Breathtaking.

"Hi," the woman said nervously. There was always something so sweet about new patients. They were so innocent, so vulnerable right when they came to her the first time. Lynn felt a tickle of excitement in her stomach.

"I'm Sarah Abbey," she continued.

Lynn rose to her feet, then reached out her hand. "Hi, Sarah. Welcome. Please, do sit down. Make yourself comfortable."

Sarah found the couch, then sat down on the edge of it. Most patients sat on the edge the first time.

"Okay, Sarah, what brings you here today?"

Her eyes met Lynn's, and she was obviously struggling.

"It's okay," Lynn said. "We're in no rush. Do take your time. You're very pretty, do you know that?"

"Really?"

"Absolutely. You're to die for."

Lynn sent her a most reassuring and slightly flirtatious smile. Just enough to make her feel that she liked her, but not so much that she knew for sure. Just enough to make her wonder and then tell herself she was a fool for thinking it. The attraction was thick between them already, and it amused Lynn. She was going to have a lot of fun with this woman; she could already feel it. At first, she'd flirt with her, but not too obviously, just enough to make her feel special, and she'd do her extra favors like let her go over time, take her in when she had a cancellation, call her if she was feeling down, send her emails to cheer her up. Stuff like that would make her depend on her. And then she'd pull it back for a little while—act distant. Make her miss it, make her desperate to get that special attention back. And that's when she'd introduce touching—a lingering hand on her arm or shoulder, a hug at the beginning of the session. Then the hug would be longer, and she'd kiss her neck and later on the lips. And Sarah wouldn't even notice how she slowly escalated things, how she manipulated her to want what she wanted. In the end, she'd beg for her to sleep with her and blame herself when it did happen. And she'd never tell anyone because she would believe it was her own fault. She did this; she wanted it.

It was a dance, and Lynn was a pro at it.

She won't know what hit her.

"It's my boyfriend," Sarah said.

Lynn nodded, then wrote on her notepad. She wasn't exactly writing what Sarah was saying, but Sarah didn't know that. She didn't know Lynn was already picturing her naked and drawing them together on the couch.

"What about him?"

"We're having some trouble."

"Oh, really? In what way?"

"He flirts with other women, and I fear he might cheat on me. I know it's probably just me in my mind, but…"

Lynn shook her head. "In here. In this space, all your feelings are valid, Sarah."

That made Sarah smile. She had a gorgeous smile, and her rosy lips were screaming to be kissed.

"Oh. Really?" Sarah asked. "Okay, then…well, so you say I am entitled to feel the way I do?"

"Absolutely. Now, tell me, what's your boyfriend's name?"

"Tommy. Tommy Waltman."

Lynn wrote the name down, this time actually writing what Lynn said because she needed the name—for later. The boyfriend was in the way. He needed to go. Plus, he was obviously hurting Sarah. Lynn would do it for her because she loved her so.

"And do you have a picture of that boyfriend of yours?" Lynn asked.

Sarah gave her a puzzled look.

"I just like to know who I'm talking about; that's all," Lynn explained. "To get the full picture, so to speak. I'm visual like that."

Sarah eased up, then nodded. "Ah, yes, of course."

Sarah grabbed her phone and scrolled through it, then turned the display to show Lynn. As she did, their hands brushed briefly, and it was like electricity through Lynn's body. She stared at the picture of the ugly boyfriend while listening to Sarah's breathing, almost unable to contain her arousal.

"Anyway," Sarah said and pulled the phone away, "I've come here to work on my jealousy issues. I think they stem from my childhood, and Tommy agrees that it would be good for me to work on them. Do you think you can help me with that?"

Lynn lifted her gaze and met Sarah's, her eyes sparkling with sexual tension.

"Absolutely. I'd like to see you weekly. I think we're in for a beautiful journey together toward your healing."

Chapter 72

"I was her patient for about a year when things started to get really weird. Lynn had always been so kind to me and seemed like she genuinely cared for me. For the first time in my life, someone actually listened to what I said, and someone actually cared and understood. It felt amazing. I had never had that."

Sarah sat up and rubbed her hands. There were still marks around her wrists from where the chains had been. Lynn had sat down on the couch, hiding her face between her hands. I was still pointing my gun at her and had called the Winter Park Police Department for backup.

"I began depending on her," Sarah continued, wiping tears from her eyes. "I trusted her and told her everything, even my deepest secrets like the fact that I was bisexual, something I had never dared to tell anyone. She then confided in me that she was too, and it was perfectly normal and nothing to be ashamed of. I felt free for the first time in my life—free to be myself. I felt better, and my jealousy issues got better since we worked out that it all stemmed from my childhood and my own father, who cheated on my mother. Lynn helped me so much, and I felt indebted to her. But there was also something else, something that made everything worse. I was very attracted to her, and she was to me as well. She flirted with me openly during our sessions and would look at me like she wanted to eat me. It was all very sexual, the atmosphere was, and what we discussed. And slowly, I began to feel worse. She started to touch me, sit on the couch with me and hold me when I cried. I didn't think it was odd since she was just comforting me, but then her hand would brush against my breast, and soon it was lingering there, touching me. I didn't stop her. I know I should have since alarms were going off inside me, yet I didn't say anything. I know I should have. But soon, she was constantly hugging me, sometimes for as long as ten-fifteen minutes. She said it was part of the therapy; it would help me heal. And then she moved on to kissing my neck, my cheek, and soon my lips. And the worst part was that I wanted it to happen. I wanted her to do it. I craved her, and soon my whole life was about her and when I would see her next. And then she started to cancel on me. Week after week, she'd come up with some excuse, and I was beginning to feel so frustrated. I longed to be with her—to feel special. It was almost like a drug. I felt like I couldn't live without her. I ended up calling her at night, crying, asking her to please see me. Finally, she did. I was back in her office, and after that, I didn't dare to say anything. I was scared I'd lose her again. The touching became more, and soon we had regular sex on the couch in her office every time I came for my appointment. And I was even paying for it, paying for every session. It felt wrong, and sometimes I'd space out when it happened. I knew it was wrong, but I didn't know how to get out of it. One day, I confided in an old friend who was visiting, telling her—I was very embarrassed—that I was having sex with my therapist. She looked at me weirdly, then said, *you don't do that kind of stuff with your doctor*. She also told me it was illegal. After finally realizing how wrong it was, I stopped coming to my sessions. I stayed away, hoping it would make it all stop, but it didn't. She started to call me constantly, telling me that I couldn't just break off my treatment—that I would end up getting even sicker. And one night, I woke up because she was hammering on my door at night. I opened it, and she grabbed me by the neck, then pushed me up against the wall behind me. Then she told me what she had done to her former clients—how she had kept his girl-friend caged in her basement, how she had murdered him afterward and pinned the murder of the girl on him. Then she told me she'd do the same to me. She'd lock me up if I didn't come back to her—to our sessions. She also threatened to send pictures of me, naked pictures of us together to my family, to my parents if I went to the police. They couldn't know I was bisexual. It would kill them. My brother is gay, and he never dared to tell them."

"So that's why you left?"

"It was the only way out. That night, I packed my stuff and left without a word to anyone, not Tommy, not my brother. I just ran away, drove to the beach, and found a small motel where I could stay. I started a new life out there, hoping she wouldn't be able to find me. How was I supposed to know she'd kill Tommy? It broke me completely when I read about it on Facebook. But I didn't even dare to come to the funeral. For all I knew, she could have killed him just to make me come out of hiding. I was scared of her. I lived every day in fear that she might show up or that she would send those pictures to my parents. I didn't dare go to the police, especially since I believed it was all my own fault. I wanted her to have sex with me. I started it myself."

I placed a hand on Sarah's shoulder. "That's what she made you believe. It's called gaslighting. When someone makes you doubt your own sanity, your own actions, and perception of the situation."

Tears filled Sarah's eyes. "I felt so awful. I thought I could start over—get a new life away from her."

"But then, somehow, she found you anyway, huh? You knew she might, and that's why you warned Scott. You feared ending up in the basement like Joanna. So, you told him to look for you if you ever disappeared. And he did. He sent me. At first, I thought he hurt you. I thought that was why you put that gun in his face, but you did it because you knew Lynn would come for you. You were trying to keep him out of it. Lynn was looking for you, and you knew that. You did it to protect him, right? Because you love him."

Sarah wiped her tears. I smiled gently.

"You can't blame yourself, Sarah. What happened with Lynn

wasn't your fault. She manipulated and groomed you. She formed an attachment that was too strong and exploited your vulnerability. She did it with other patients, too; she made them fulfill her own needs. She made you want her. She made you feel like you were in love with her. She knew better than to do that. As a therapist, she knows about transference—when the patient thinks they're in love with their therapist, but really, it's an unmet need from her child-hood, usually from a parent that she's projecting upon the therapist. It's perfectly normal. Lynn should have known better. Instead, she nourished it and made it grow so strong so her patients would do anything for her. What she wanted became what you wanted, and then she could have her way with you. But it's over now, Sarah," I said. "It's all over now."

Sarah looked up at me with relief in her eyes, and for one unfor-givable second, I let my eyes wander away from Lynn on the couch to meet Sarah's glare. When I saw the fear striking Sarah's eyes as her look fell on what was behind me, it was too late.

Chapter 73

There was a tray on the coffee table. It was made of thick glass and held floral decorations. Lynn had gotten ahold of it, and, seconds later, she smashed it into the back of my head. The pain felt like an explosion, and I saw white before my eyes as I crumpled to my knees. I didn't even feel the gun being taken out of my hand, but it wasn't there when I finally came to myself again. Confused, I lifted my hurting head, felt the blood on the back, then saw Sarah being dragged across the floor by the hair while she was screaming. I could hear the screams, but it sounded like she was underwater. It took me a few seconds to compose myself just enough to react. By then, I saw that the sledgehammer was gone, and as I stumbled to my feet, fear jolting through my body, I saw the hammer being lifted in the kitchen, swung through the air, and I heard it fall, hitting something below, crushing something.

Or someone.

I screamed.

"NO!"

I jolted forward, rushing ahead, then felt dizzy and tripped over my own feet, falling flat before I managed to get up again and push myself forward, heart throbbing, tears springing to my eyes.

Oh, my God. She killed Sarah. She killed her!

I saw the blood as I came closer and could barely breathe. I saw Lynn standing above her, one foot on either side of Sarah's hips, still holding the end of the sledgehammer. I was blinking my eyes to see correctly as my sight was still blurry, and it felt like I was in the middle of a dream. Narrowing my eyes to better focus, I looked for the other end of the hammer. It was lodged in Sarah's torso, in her shoulder as she had tried to roll away just as it came down on her. The shoulder looked to be in an odd position, dislocated, and now Sarah was screaming.

But screaming meant she was alive.

The question was for how long.

Lynn didn't seem to have noticed me. She was focused on her task and pulled the hammer back up into the air, getting herself ready to swing it at Sarah again. Sarah was screaming like a wounded animal, and I knew that she wouldn't be able to move this time. Her shoulder had been crushed. She was frozen in pain, maybe even drifting into unconsciousness. Meanwhile, the hammer lingered in the air above her as Lynn got ready to let it fall on her again.

What do I do?

I did the only thing I could do. I gathered myself, then stormed with everything I had, all I knew how to, toward her. I blasted into her by her hips and pushed her away. Lynn screamed, and the hammer was dropped, falling on my arm hard. I tumbled on top of Lynn, screaming in pain as she kicked and pushed me, trying to get me off her.

She got to her feet, then went for the gun she had put on the kitchen counter while I struggled to get back up, my arm pounding. When I finally got up, she was standing in front of me with the gun pointed at me. Her nostrils were flaring, her eyes manic.

She didn't even say anything.

She simply pulled the trigger.

But right when she did, somehow, Sarah had gotten herself onto her feet and managed to grab a plate on the counter and throw it at her. The plate hit Lynn straight in the face, causing her to fall back right when the gun went off. The bullet whistled through the air and hit the cabinets behind me.

A second later, I was on top of Lynn, pinning her down with my one good arm. I sat on her—not letting her move an inch—until the police and EMTs arrived.

Chapter 74

It was four in the morning before I finally made it back home, my arm heavily bandaged. It wasn't fractured, they told me at the hospital, and I had suffered a concussion from the hit with the glass tray, but I was good to go home if I made sure I got a lot of rest. I wasn't sure I could live up to that promise with two babies in the house, but I didn't tell the doctor that.

I opened my front door and stepped into the living room, feeling all kinds of exhausted. I threw my keys on the small table by the door, turned on the lights, then gasped, startled.

"Matt?"

He was sitting in the recliner, staring at me.

"Gosh, you scared me," I said, clasping my chest.

He didn't wince. He stared at me, his eyes dark and sinister.

"I waited for you," he said.

I looked at him, trying to figure out what he was talking about.

"Oh, no," I said as the dime dropped. "You went to Pompano's?"

He nodded. "I waited three hours. I called you and texted you, but nothing."

I looked at the display on my phone. It was pitch black.

"It died hours ago," I said. "That's why I didn't call from the hospital. Plus, I knew you were all probably sleeping. I wanted to tell you everything in the morning. I didn't have time to call earlier or text you back. It was a matter of life and death."

"It always is, isn't it?" he said.

I approached him with an exhale. I rubbed my forehead. "All right, maybe I could have called you back. I did see that you had tried to reach me earlier, but to be honest, I didn't want to fight with you, and I didn't have time to explain what was going on. I didn't want you to get mad at me. I had promised not to deal with this case anymore. I just couldn't, Matt. You must understand that. I can't *not* care."

"Just not about those that love you."

"That's not fair, Matt."

"It's not?"

I sat down in the recliner in front of him. I could hear my dad snoring lightly by the fireplace. They were leaving in the morning. I was looking forward to getting the house back, but I was sad to see them go.

"I found Sarah Abbey tonight, Matt. I was right. She was in great danger. I actually saved her if it's of any interest."

"That's great."

"Yeah, well, she got badly hurt, and they're not sure her shoulder will ever be normal again, but she's alive. She and Scott can be reunited. You do know that's what this was all about, right?"

"I've had my doubts."

I stared at him while remembering the kiss Scott and I had shared. I didn't like how much I thought about it. It wasn't so much the kiss, or Scott, as it was the fact that I had let it happen and enjoyed it.

I leaned back in the recliner.

"Anyway, it's over now. I handed the case over to the Winter Park Police Department, and I am letting it go now. Everything can get back to normal."

He lifted his eyebrows.

"Normal? And just exactly what is that? Please, tell me because I honestly don't know."

I stared at him, scrutinizing him. I guess you could say I was looking for what I had fallen in love with in the first place.

I couldn't find it.

"You know what?" I said.

His eyes met mine. "No, but I have a feeling you'll tell me."

"I am sick of this."

He threw out his arms. "Me too."

"I am sick and tired of having the same fight over and over again," I said. "And to be honest, I can't really find the reason to keep going."

He paused, his eyes scrutinizing me.

"What are you saying?"

His lips slightly quivered when he said it. He thought I didn't notice.

"I'm saying that I think you should move out—you and Elijah. I need time to think. I need to figure out what it is I really want because it's not this. I have rushed from one relationship, which ended in a bad divorce, and thrown myself directly into your arms, and I am beginning to think it was too soon."

Matt stared at me, not blinking.

"So…you're calling off the wedding?"

I exhaled, feeling good about my decision for once.

"I guess that's what I am saying."

A strange scoff left Matt's mouth, and he shook his head at me. He rose to his feet and walked past me, mumbling.

"I can't believe you."

Then, he left, slamming the front door behind him so hard my dad woke up and came out to me, rubbing his unshaven face, squinting his eyes at me.

"Eva Rae? What's going on? Why are you sitting here? What happened to your arm, sweetie? Are you okay?

I looked up at him, then nodded. "You know what? I think I am. I think I have finally taken control of my own life. It's a mess and chaotic at times—well, most of the time. But it's the way I like it. I don't do normal."

That made my dad smile. He placed a hand on my shoulder while nodding.

"Good for you, sweetie. Good for you."

He waited for a few seconds, then added, "Do you want a beer or something?"

I laughed, then shook my head.

"No. I need to sleep. There are only a few hours till the two little monsters will wake up. But thanks."

Epilogue

Chapter 75

The sound of the Ring doorbell rang in the hall inside. I could see movement behind the frosted glass with the beautiful palm trees. The door was opened, and a face appeared.

"Kim."

"Eva Rae? What are you doing here?" Kim said and stepped outside, closing the door behind her while whispering, "You can't be here."

"Yes, I can," I said and stepped aside. "And I haven't come alone."

Kim's eyes fell on the two women behind me.

"This is my sister, Sydney, and this is Mrs. Harris, from the Department for Children and Families."

Kim's eyes grew big. "DCF? But…"

"We're here to talk to Amy."

"But…Amy is…"

"Save it. We know she's in there, and we know you've been keeping her away from her child."

Out of the corner of my eye, I looked at my minivan, knowing that inside of it sat Christine, keeping an eye on Owen until we came back out, hopefully with Amy.

"We have done no such…"

"Kim," I said. "Let us in, please."

Her shoulders slumped, and she became resigned. "Okay. But make it brief. If Phil finds out you've…"

We didn't listen to the rest of that sentence but walked right past her into the massive hall.

"Where is she?" I asked. "Upstairs?"

Kim nodded. "In her room."

I rushed up the stairs, Sydney and Mrs. Harris coming up right behind me. We opened one door, and I called her name, but that was a bathroom. I grabbed the handle of the next door and shook it.

"It's locked."

I knocked.

"Amy?"

"Y-yes?" a small, thin voice said behind it. "Is anyone there? Is that you, Eva Rae? Please, help me."

My heart dropped as the realization sank in. "They're keeping her locked up."

"This is serious," Mrs. Harris said.

"Please, help me," Amy said.

Mrs. Harris faced Kim. She spoke with a firm voice yet failed to hide how angry she really was.

"Please, open the door, Mrs. Robinson."

Kim walked up and put the key in the door without protest. She turned it, and it opened. I pushed the door open. Amy threw herself into my arms. I grabbed her and held her tight, kissing her hair.

"Oh, you poor thing. You poor, poor child."

She cried and held me tight like she didn't want me ever to let go of her again. "Is he all right? How's Owen?"

I nodded, crying heavily. "He's fine. He's just fine."

Amy relaxed, but I didn't let go of her. My heart was breaking for the girl.

"I meant to come back," she said, sobbing. "On the day I ran away, I came here to ask my mom to forgive me and for her help, but then my dad came home, and he…he grabbed me, then dragged me into my room and locked the door. I couldn't get out. I couldn't get back to Owen."

"I know, sweetie. I know. It's okay." I paused, then took a deep breath before I asked what had been on my mind for quite some time, "He's the father, isn't he? Your father? He's Owen's father, right?"

Amy's body jolted in sobs, and I held her so she wouldn't fall to her knees. "Oh, my God," she said. "Oh, my God."

"It's okay, Amy. I've got you now. He can't hurt you or Owen anymore."

"He was so angry," she said between sobs. "When it turned out that I was pregnant, and my mother…she wouldn't forgive me. That's why I ran away. They wanted me to get rid of him, but how could I? They said my dad might end up in jail if anyone found out, and that made me feel guilty, but in the end, I had to protect my child."

I exchanged a look with Mrs. Harris, grabbed Amy by the shoulders, and looked into her eyes.

"It's not your fault, Amy. Do you hear me? He's the one to blame. Everything is going to be all right. We're taking you home now."

"But…where are you taking her?" Kim asked.

"Sydney and I run a shelter for young women who have been trafficked. We have a team of doctors and psychiatrists that can help her get her life back together again. She'll be taken care of there."

"But…but what am I supposed to tell Phil when he comes home?" Kim asked as we started walking down the stairs.

I turned and looked at her. She seemed so lost; it was heartbreaking. But she had chosen her life, and now she had to live it. I didn't feel sorry for her. Phil was going to jail for what he had done, and she would end up very lonely.

"I'm sure you'll think of something."

Then, I turned away and put my arm around Amy, walking her out to her son in my car. When she saw him, her face lit up, and tears sprang to her eyes. She took him out of the carrier, then held him close.

"Oh, my sweet boy. I am never letting go of you again. Do you hear me? Never. Nothing and no one will ever come between us again."

I placed a hand on her shoulder, fighting to press the tears back, but failing miserably.

"It's time. We need to go."

Chapter 76

"You're telling me you would sit here in your car and watch her? While she was in her house? No wonder she thought you were creepy and called the cops on you."

I looked at Scott, sitting next to me in my minivan. I had parked it across the street from Lily Mitchell's house. He had called me the day before and asked me to help him out with one more favor—just this one favor. Once he had explained to me what it was, I couldn't say no to him.

"There she is," he said and pointed. "Look at her; isn't she gorgeous?"

I exhaled and nodded, then placed a hand on his shoulder.

"Let's do this."

He took in a deep, nervous breath, and I got out of the car. I walked toward Lily, who was hurrying to her car in the driveway while searching her purse for her keys.

"Excuse me? Lily?"

She stopped. Her green eyes landed on me. "Yes? Can I help you?"

I glanced briefly toward Scott in the car across the street, and she saw me do it, then went pale.

"No, no, it's him again."

I reached out my hand. "It's okay, Lily."

"No, it's not. He's been stalking me, and he's a creep. I have a restraining order out on him. He's got some nerve showing up like this again."

"Lily, listen to me…"

She pulled out her phone from her purse. "I'm calling the police."

I placed a hand on her arm to stop her, then looked her deep in the eyes. "Lily, you need to listen to me. You'll want to, okay?"

She lowered the phone, her eyes scrutinizing me. "Why should I trust you? You're with him, aren't you?"

"Just hear me out," I said. "Then you can call the cops afterward, okay?"

She contemplated for a second, then nodded. "All right. I'll hear what you have to say."

I breathed, relieved, then pointed toward Scott. "That guy over there *has* been stalking you; you're right about that."

She crossed her arms in front of her chest. "Okay, and?"

"And you're right that he has been acting very creepy toward you…"

"So, now that we've stated the obvious, I'm still waiting for the good part…"

I grabbed her shoulders. "Lily. That man over there has a very special reason for wanting to see you. He's been trying to find the courage to approach you and tell you something very important."

Lily's eyes looked like they didn't believe me at first, then eased up. A furrow grew between her brows.

"Tell me something? Like what?"

I exhaled. "He's…Lily…he's your father."

She pulled back. "Excuse me?"

I bit my lip, then nodded. "He only just recently found out himself. That's why he has been following you. He was trying to find a way to tell you. He wants to talk to you and tell you more himself, but…well, he can't as long as you're scared of him."

She swallowed. I saw tears well up in her eyes as she looked at

Scott, who had stepped out of the car and stood in the street, staring at us.

"Are you telling me that...that...that man...the creep is my father?"

I nodded. "Yes. He didn't know he had a daughter until six months ago when his old girlfriend—your mother—died and her mother—your grandmother—contacted him to let him know. All he wants is to get to know you. Do you think you can find room for him in your heart?"

Lily stared at Scott, and in that second, I could suddenly see just how much the two of them looked alike. It was uncanny. The angled nose, the green eyes, and even the small furrow between the eyes when they were worried or confused.

Lily took a step closer to him, narrowing her eyes, studying Scott. Scott remained still, but I could see his hands were shaking badly as she approached him slowly. She stood close to him, studying him from top to bottom with a skeptical look. Scott smiled nervously.

"You're...supposed to be my dad?"

He nodded.

"Do you have any proof of that?"

He shrugged. "We can do a DNA test if you like. If that'll make you feel better."

She paused. "Maybe. You sure are handsome enough for my mother to fall for you."

That made Scott smile. Tears were springing to his eyes, and his torso was shaking.

"Okay," Lily said, nodding. "I will trust you for now. But we're doing that test just in case."

"So...can I see you sometime?"

She looked at him. "You can take me to lunch next week. Then I'll have called the police and retracted the restraining order."

Scott eased up. His shoulders came down, and now he was smiling blissfully like only a father gazing upon his daughter could look. She gave him another glance, then turned on her high-heeled

Doc Martin boots, and walked past me, yelling after him, "But you're paying; don't forget that."

"I won't!" he yelled back.

"And bring the big checkbook because I want lobster!"

That made Scott laugh.

"That's my daughter," he said, tears in his eyes as she drove away. I hugged him and held him tight.

"No doubt about it," I said.

I pulled out of the hug, and Scott grabbed my face between his hands. "Thank you so much for all you have done for me."

I blushed. Being this close to him again made my stomach flutter.

"No problem. What are friends for, right?"

He looked into my eyes, and I felt myself go soft.

"I'd say we're a little more than that, wouldn't you?" he said.

I scoffed. "Don't flatter yourself."

He tilted his head and leaned in for a kiss. Seeing this, I felt a huge desire to lean into it too, but I stopped myself.

"No, Scott," I whispered. "We can't do this."

"Why not? You and Matt have split up. Sarah and I are over. I'll be moving out soon. I realized I'm still in love with you."

That was a little too much for me, and I pulled away. "What are you talking about, Scott?"

"I'm crazy about you, Eva Rae. I always was."

"I don't know what to say to that."

"Tell me you're crazy about me too," Scott said, grabbing my chin and pulling it up.

I shook my head. "I...I don't know, Scott."

"At least let me see you again."

I shook my head and took a step away from him. "Not now. I need time to think. I rushed into things with Matt right after my marriage ended. I never really sat down and thought about what I wanted. There's a lot I need to figure out, but right now, I just want to be there for my family, for my children."

He nodded, eyes disappointed. "Okay. But call me when you're done thinking."

"We'll see. I need to go now. Angel will wake up from her nap soon. Do you need to be dropped off somewhere?"

He shook his head, then looked down, putting his hands in his pockets.

"I'll grab an Uber home. You go ahead."

I left him standing there on the asphalt, looking after me as I got into my car while he waited for his ride. Our eyes locked as I drove past him, standing there, looking like a child who had just lost his toy.

I felt good about my decision as I drove up DeLeon Road toward my home. Alex and Olivia were goofing around outside on the lawn, spraying each other with the hose. Olivia grabbed Alex, lifted him in the air, and then stuck the hose into his pants until he screamed for mercy. Seeing them made me laugh, and I parked in the driveway while Alex ran up to me.

"Mo-o-o-om, Olivia is bullying me."

I hugged my soaking son and held him in my arms, then kissed him until he complained and wanted to be put down.

"He had it coming, you know," Olivia said, still laughing.

"I know," I said while Alex ran back in.

I put my arm around my oldest daughter's shoulder as we walked back inside, realizing this was the best I had felt in years.

THE END

Afterword

Dear Reader,

Thank you for purchasing *To Die For (Eva Rae Thomas #8)*.

The idea for this book actually came to me when I started therapy myself.

I was going through some really rough things from my past that I needed help to deal with and found an amazing therapist, who is nothing like the one in this book, naturally. But it was while going through my sessions with her that I thought, *what if a therapist let someone go too far?*

What if she herself wasn't really all there? How wrong could it go?

And then I let it go really, really wrong.

That was fun.

Now, I am still in therapy, and she has been helping me a lot, so this book is in no way a reflection of reality, but it was fun to write.

Take care,

Willow

About the Author

Willow Rose is a multi-million-copy best-selling Author and an Amazon ALL-star Author of more than 80 novels.

Several of her books have reached the top 10 of ALL books on Amazon in the US, UK, and Canada. She has sold more than six million books all over the world.

She writes Mystery, Thriller, Paranormal, Romance, Suspense, Horror, Supernatural thrillers, and Fantasy.

Willow's books are fast-paced, nail-biting pageturners with twists you won't see coming. That's why her fans call her The Queen of Plot Twists.

Willow lives on Florida's Space Coast with her husband and two daughters. When she is not writing or reading, you will find her surfing and watch the dolphins play in the waves of the Atlantic Ocean.

Tired of too many emails? Text the word: "willowrose" to 31996 to sign up to Willow's VIP text List to get a text alert with news about New Releases, Giveaways, Bargains and Free books from Willow.

CPSIA information can be obtained
at www.ICGtesting.com
Printed in the USA
LVHW092059140621
689902LV00017B/311/J

9 781954 938090